Reviews for Wildflower Witch

-Lovely, gentle read, full of love and understanding of nature. The natural way of things that are so often missing in today's times.

-What a wonderful book. I enjoyed every word. A lovely cosy story with enchanting characters. I look forward to reading more in this series. Sit back and enjoy

-A pleasure for the senses and informative as well. A delightful weaving together of a number of threads. Well crafted storyline with well rounded characters. Highly recommended.

-Beautiful, magical story. I absolutely love this book. Believable real witches, a hint of otherworldly fae, a wonderful rural setting, lovable animal characters. Just the sort of story I love.

-I honestly don't know how to explain how this book makes me feel. It's left a real yearning for "if only". I read it within thirty six hours and look forward so much to her other books.

-Brilliant. I've read a few of this author's books and so I know she doesn't disappoint. However, this really exceeded my expectations. It was the best book of hers yet. Need more of this story please.

-Susanna, may I say that you have achieved what you set out to do. I read your book in a day when I needed a feel good relaxation for mind and body which ended with a smile on my face, looking for more of your writing. Thank you

CHANTER'S HILL

The Witches of Farstone Moor –
Book 2

Susanna Scott

For Lisa,
My daughter and my best friend.
With love.

"Witchcraft is a way of life–not a belief system, not a religion, not a protest against Christianity. It is a recognition of the Earth itself and of ourselves as part of the Earth."

Janet and Stewart Farrar: The Chroniclers of Modern Witchcraft.

Chapter 1

It was a cold, wet, grey winter's day in late October and snowflakes were just starting to fall. The weather matched Ailsa McKendry's mood.

It was all her Aunt Philippa's fault that she had been torn away up North from her cosy, warm little flat in Crossgates, to come to this god-forsaken corner of the North Yorkshire Moors. No wonder her mother and father had left the area when she was ten years old.

The estate agent got out of the car reluctantly and waited for her to follow him. He took the opportunity to hand over his card.

'For when you need to sell your flat, we'd be happy to handle it for you.'

She took it silently, thinking that he probably wouldn't be too happy if he saw it. Her rose-tinted glasses of a few moments earlier were being replaced by reality. The flat was pokey, damp and for 'little' think 'no room to swing a cat'. Ailsa wondered how people tested these things out. Did they take a cat, swing it round by its tail, then give it a can of Whiskas and a catnip mouse to compensate?

Looking up at the place in front of her, Nightowl's Hide, she could see both why it should be hidden and why it would have far more damp problems than her flat. It was almost derelict. Why on earth had Aunt Philippa recommended this? Then she remembered, it had six acres of land behind it and Philippa knew it was land that Ailsa needed.

As Mr DBS Bullen, Property Agent, according to his card, attempted a police-style forced entry on the jammed door, rubbing his shoulder in pain afterwards, she realised it was a long time since anyone had been shown around this property. As she stepped inside to be met with just one large, decrepit room, she knew why. It seemed to incorporate kitchen, dining room and living room, but as there was no furniture or any fixtures for that matter, it was difficult to judge.

'Is this the only room?' she asked incredulously.

'Yes,' he sighed, obviously answering the question for the twentieth time, 'but there are six acres with it.'

She nodded and he frowned.

'You do want six acres?'

'Yes.'

'What would you do with them?'

'I would demolish this place and rebuild a little further back from the road for a start.'

'Mmm' he said.

'In cottage style, in keeping with the other stone cottages in the village,' she revised.

'I see,' he said, pretending to look through his appointment book. If he told her the truth, she'd never buy it. He could have sold it at least five times if it hadn't been for...

'I can't demolish it, can I?' She narrowed her eyes at him.

'No' he coughed.

'Why?'

'It's a building of historical importance. I don't see why, as it was only some old witch who lived in it centuries ago. If you even *believe* in witches.'

Witches! Now she could understand her aunt's enthusiasm about her buying this place. Farstone, Philippa's village and the village where Ailsa was born, was also the birthplace of the Witches of Farstone legend. It was that which had forced her parents to leave the village. Although Philippa, who still lived there and ran the local Inn, The Peverel Arms, denied this. It was 'that woman's' fault, she had said, having admitted to never liking her sister-in-law. She was also annoyed at Ailsa for taking her mother's maiden name of McKendry as her stage name, although Ailsa just chose it as it sounded better than Reed. She had thought, as Hatton-le-Hollow was twenty miles away from Farstone, that she had left all thoughts of witches behind. Obviously, they were following her around.

No, this place wasn't for her. Why had Philippa made her travel two hundred miles to see this place on the say-so of Binky Peverel, the local seer? Ailsa had arrived at the inn at 9:00 p.m. last night. Then, after a full English breakfast in the morning, she had to dash here, look around, make a decision, then get back tonight for a meeting in Crossgates first thing tomorrow. Well, she had made her decision. This definitely wasn't for her.

'Do you want to see upstairs?' he almost whispered as he glanced at her set features. She looked at a ladder leading to a half-floor above.

'No.'

'It could be made into two bedrooms.'

'And is there a modern ensuite bathroom hiding there too?'

She smiled like a tiger before catching its prey. A small shake of the head was his answer.

'But the land. You'd like to see the land?'

'No thank you.'

'Admittedly, it wouldn't look its best on a day like today and it's a fair old walk up to the top in this bad weather.'

He wasn't exactly relishing it himself, but this stopped Ailsa in her tracks. She remembered the land area plans that Philippa had sent to her. If she had got it right, the land was in a long strip behind the cottage, which increased gradually from immediately behind the cottage to become much wider towards the top. She had to ignore the Hide itself because the land was exactly what she wanted and she doubted she would be able to get the same land for the remarkably cheap price that this was advertised for. She now realised why it was so cheap, of course, but still...

'Yes, let's have a look at the land then' she eventually answered.

Mr. DBS Bullen shoulders sagged. He thought of a pint in a warm pub in Pickering and reluctantly put his collar up and pulled down his countryman's flat hat over his eyes.

*

They headed outside under a strange pink and grey sky. Living most of her thirty-five years in a city, she couldn't know the country way of reading the weather, but even she knew that a pink sky at midday wasn't a good sign. There was more snow on the way and she was dreading the journey home.

Even as she thought of the word home, she realised that her tiny eighth-floor flat had never been home. She wondered against her will, if this forgotten piece of property ever could be that home.

As they walked slowly up the overgrown land, he in his regulation Hunter's wellies and she in her Doc Martens, she fell quiet. DBS kept glancing at her, expecting questions, but none came, so he fell silent too.

There were high hedges on each side, screening out the neighbours near the road. There was a pub to the left of the Hide, separated by a wide driveway and there was a small stone cottage to the right. The hedges could be cut down neatly and precisely, but thought Ailsa, they provided privacy, so why would she? The neighbours might want them neatened a little, which was fair enough, but otherwise they could stay as they were. The hedges continued widening out with the land and were still at least eight feet high. The land was marked out at intervals with wild-looking plants, shrubs and the foundations of what could have been small barns or workshops. Nothing recognisable though.

'What has the land been used for?'

He jumped physically, not expecting her voice.

'It was – well -we're not sure. We think it was used for grazing animals a lot of the time. Sheep possibly. It has been rented out to local farmers in the past.'

She looked satisfied. Buoyed up by this, he said,

'The pigeons have also used the cottage to roost. You probably noticed pigeon poo on the-' he stopped seeing her steely gaze.

'I haven't,' she said, continuing her walk up the land, 'but I will make a note to do so before I go.' DBS was beginning to hate his job.

Apart from trees dotted around at the edges, it was mostly grassland, which was fine by her. She wondered if those farmers would graze their sheep free of charge again to get the grass down, then wondered why she was thinking of it in a personal way, as if it mattered, as if it were already hers. The further up they walked, the more she could feel her heart quickening and her soul melting in opposition to her first thoughts.

At the end of the land, at its widest, was a strange building. A large barn, almost as dilapidated as the cottage. Was that wattle and daub at the bottom of it? It was unlike anything she had seen. It was round and the roof had previously been thatched but hardly anything was left now, apart from partial beams with very old, dirty thatch clinging to them.

The most preserved part was a large wooden entrance like a very high, wide porch with no door. She went inside and stood in the centre. A strange feeling of peace came over her as though all the worries on her shoulders had fallen away. After a few minutes, she came out.

'What is this?' she asked, 'it wasn't on the plans.'

'Only an old barn. Now, I imagine this *can* be demolished' he smiled, glad to have some good news.

'You are joking' she shot back. 'This is the best part of the deal.'

He looked confused.

'So does that mean you want to buy the place? he ventured.

She turned to face him. Buy this dilapidated heap of stone decorated with pigeon poo with its overgrown grass and hedges with another dilapidated building at the bottom of it?

'I think it does' she said, then worried that DBS was going into a state of shock, so she smiled and it seemed to make things worse. He recovered quickly, albeit with a look of disbelief on his face and they started to walk back.

She turned to look once more at the round barn, which was when she caught sight, through the driving sleet now almost blinding them, of the hill at the back of the barn, right at the top of the land. It was behind a low, partially collapsed wall, so it didn't look like it was on her land. It was a small-ish, mound-shaped hill, not more than twelve feet at its highest point but at least three times that in diameter. On this hill was a circular stand of trees, hiding the top itself from sight. It fascinated her.

She realised she had been staring at the hill for a while after she heard a cough from DBS and a plaintive whine.

'Shall we head back, Miss McKendry?'

'What is that hill? Is it mine?' she asked.

'I don't think so' he said, rifling through his papers and trying to stop them getting wet. He pulled out an A4 sheet. 'It's included in the area land survey, but strangely, I don't think it's part of the deal' He looked closely at the paper.

'It's called Chanter's Hill,' he said.

Chapter 2

It was now almost five months later and the journey up to Yorkshire was much better than Ailsa's last trip. The sun was shining for a start, making everything better, even though the days were hovering between warm and 'fair nithering'.

She had been to Hatton-le-Hollow twice since she had made the rash decision to buy Nightowl's Hide. Once in mid-November, when she had a crisis meeting with council planners, developers and builders. The second time was to visit the cottage itself with her builders in early December, where all there was to see was the back wall standing. A vast improvement, she thought.

At that point, she had wondered what perverse impulse had made her buy it in the first place. A walk up to the top of the land had given her the answer and calmed her strained nerves. Now there were less than fifty miles to go, so she pulled off the main moor road to a cafe down the lane, with an arrow pointing to an invisible 'Bette's Cafe. Good food snacks drinks.' Not good punctuation though. She needed a rest before facing her family.

She had promised to stay overnight at the Peverel Arms with Philippa, Jerry and her cousin Mary. She didn't know why she was so sniffy about them and the village of Farstone. Thinking about it over the last few months, she realised she was being influenced by her mother's attitude. Jane Reed had never got on with Philippa and she had been the one who wanted to get away from the place. Her father, Kenneth, Philippa's brother, didn't want to go at first, but as usual, fell in with what his opinionated wife decreed. It was all incidental now as their marriage had broken up when Ailsa had left home to get her own place.

They'd been waiting to separate for a long time; it was obvious. The last few years before she was eighteen were a living hell for Ailsa, with all the shouting, mostly on her mother's part, it had to be said. She knew she was opinionated like her mother, but she hoped she was more like her father. He was gentle and kind, which showed far more after their divorce than before it. Ailsa had also inherited his blue eyes and his hair colour, which was the colour of straw, like most of the Reeds. Hers fell about her shoulders, long and wavy. At least it wasn't black like the Gardwickes. Now they did look like witches.

Bette, if indeed that was the plump, grey-haired lady behind the counter, served her a scone and a cup of tea without a smile. The surroundings were spartan. Ailsa wondered how many customers she would get. She must be bored out of her mind most of the time. She certainly looked it. However, the tea was good and hot and the scone was fresh and tasty with plenty of butter. So she sat and stared out into a line of trees through which she could see a field beyond.

Shoots were beginning to come through. It would be the first day of Spring soon. Bette came over unasked with a refill from the huge teapot. Ailsa warmed towards her and smiled - and earned a flicker of a smile back.

She reflected on her metaphorical journey to get here. The fights on the phone with the local authorities and the county planning department had seemed insurmountable. So much so that she was surprised she had reached this stage in less than five months. There was a long way to go, but she had made a start. The Historic Buildings committee, debating whether the Hide was a building of local historic interest, had been easier. The title had been granted just before the Second World War and had never been questioned. They visited the site and, as the building was basically a shell with nothing of value inside, they had no objections to a new rebuild. Both the Historic Buildings and the other wider authorities agreed that the back wall should be left standing and incorporated into the rebuilding.

There were no other features to preserve. No wood panelling, no ancient fireplace. Only a hole at the bottom of a chimney which had fallen away, the broken remains of an old sink, fallen to the floor and definitely no internal features like cornicing, sweeping staircases or parquet flooring. It was essentially, as she had first thought, a one-room cottage or a small hovel, depending on which way you looked at it. Fitting accommodation for the witch at that time, she supposed, if such a witch had ever existed.

Gallipot Cottage in Farstone had been built up and extended from one room into a larger cottage with more rooms, which is what she herself intended. The Hide hadn't been lived in for centuries. Possibly the village witch of local history was its last inhabitant - one Effie Scritchell, according to a know-it-all local. There had probably been straw on the floor and the half floor had been used for storage. If the witch had any sense, she'd have slept in front of the embers of the fireplace downstairs.

There were hardly any grumblings from the neighbours. They probably wanted to see the eyesore replaced. She didn't want to get off on the wrong foot so emails passed between her and the one member of the local community who seemed to have a problem with it, the know-it-all local, a Mrs. Pennyquick, who was a retired teacher.

Things came to a head on the rebuilding when she asked Mrs. Pennyquick to go around and look at the place and tell her if *she* could live there as it was. The next day, obviously realising the truth of Ailsa's words, Mrs. Pennyquick fired many questions at Ailsa.

Ailsa had already asked her if it could be Nightowl's Cottage instead, but Mrs. Pennyquick said it was Hide for a reason, neglecting to tell her what that reason was. She asked if Ailsa was going to live there permanently, making the village her home. Was the building going to be in keeping with the rest of the village? Would she promise to keep the stone figure of an owl on the land at Nightowl's Hide? Lastly, would she try and preserve what she could?

She could answer yes to the first few questions and promised to try for the last one. In the end, this came down to reusing as much stone as she could in the new building, which she had already decided to do to reduce costs anyway and strangely, she found herself promising to incorporate the broken pieces of the sink into a mosaic outside. The idea had bizarrely popped into her mind. It was no skin off her nose anyway.

When Mrs. P. had told her sternly in yet another phone call that she Must Not Demolish the round barn, Ailsa's hackles rose. She told her in the same tone of voice but with an edge to it, that she had No Intention of getting rid of the round barn and in her opinion it was the best thing there, being the main reason she had bought the place. There had been silence at the other end, so Ailsa continued to tell her that she would probably rethatch it and rebuild it sympathetically to how it would have been, keeping what she could of the original.

A chuckle came through the phone. 'I can see you're going to be a force to be reckoned with', said the amused voice before she rang off.

The property manager, Ade, who headed the local builders, carpenters and plasterers - they were all related. Nepotism was alive and well in these parts- had sent a photo which showed an almost habitable cottage. So she was hoping after the night at the inn that she could at least sleep, shower and boil a kettle there. Perhaps she could even use a microwave.

*

'Ailsa Reed.'

Ailsa turned as she walked across the inn's car park in Farstone.

'Peggy Harker,' she replied, looking at the old woman with a halo of frizzy silver hair. She wasn't smiling but that was normal for Peggy. She remembered being a little scared of her when she was young and things hadn't changed much.

'Here to visit your aunt, are you?'

'Just a flying visit overnight, then I'm–' she didn't see why she should tell Peggy her business. 'then I'm staying elsewhere.'

Peggy nodded slowly.

'At Effie Scritchell's place, I hear.'

Did she honestly think she could keep anything from Peggy? News travelled fast in these isolated villages with nothing else to do but gossip.

'You heard right,' she conceded and continued to walk into the Peverel Arms.

Peggy walked on up towards Peverel Hall. Probably going to one of her witch meetings at the Folly, Ailsa scoffed. She and her friends had spied on them when they were young, but hadn't seen anyone turned into a toad. Although one of Peggy's sour glances in their direction still made them think it was a distinct possibility.

'Ailsa, welcome back, love.' The plump figure of Philippa Reed came out from behind the bar and enveloped her in a bear hug. A squeak from the kitchen doorway announced her cousin Mary's presence before she, too, ran over to Ailsa for a hug. Jerry, her uncle and Mary's dad and Philippa's partner, was an incomer. He gave her a cheery wave, then went behind the bar, ready to take over from Philippa. There were only a few walkers in just now.

'Come through to the back. You must be hungry' said Philippa. It didn't matter what time of the day it was, her aunt always assumed she would be hungry.

'Well–'

'No, tell you what' she said in the unique Yorkshire accent they spoke around here. 'You can sit next to the fire in the snug now. Jerry, get Ailsa a drink.'

The walkers who were in the process of vacating their fireside table looked slightly alarmed at having their seats taken over before they had zipped up their coats. Jerry brought a cider across to her table and smiled quietly. They say chalk and cheese thrive well in relationships. That was the case with her aunt and uncle. They were still happy as far as Ailsa could see.

As all four of them finished off their hot-pots in the deserted pub. The door opened and a tall dark-haired and beautiful young woman walked in, followed closely by a taller, darker-haired and if possible, even more gorgeous and striking-looking man. Ah, thought Ailsa at this point, it must be the mythical Flora Gardwicke and Calum Hythe.

This was the lady who had rejuvenated the Witches of Farstone and brought her partner Cal into the bosom of the village from his lonely life upon the moors. She wasn't sure she was happy about Flora reviving what she saw as an outmoded legend, but the woman coming over to her with her arms outstretched and a warm smile won her over straight away. There were a few more hugs before Jerry and Cal went over to the bar to get a round in. Flora took off her coat before she sat down.

'Congratulations,' smiled Ailsa.

 Flora looked puzzled.

'To both of you on the...'

Oh God, she'd obviously put her foot in it.

'And I didn't think I was showing yet!'

Ailsa looked at Flora's slim figure. She didn't know what she was thinking. Why had it even occurred to her?

'Unless...' And Flora looked at Philippa, who had a strange, wide-eyed expression on her face.

'I-I might have let something slip,' her aunt stammered.

Ailsa contemplated pretending she had a sudden migraine and needed her bed.

'It doesn't matter anyway, we're very proud and very happy to let everyone know we're expecting a baby,' grinned Cal proudly as he set the drinks down.

'We certainly are,' smiled Flora, grabbing hold of Ailsa's hand and squeezing it, 'especially members of our extended family.'

Ailsa remembered now that there was some connection between the Reeds and the Gardwickes from way back. Although it was so long ago that whatever tenuous link there was between them had been forgotten.

'When is it due?' Ailsa asked Flora.

'In August, if things go according to plan.' She took a quiet sip of her lime and soda while Cal looked at her lovingly. Ailsa remembered then that there had been something about Flora's own mother dying while giving birth to her. This was obviously playing on Flora's mind.

In the course of the evening, all awkwardness became forgotten as new projects were discussed and questions asked about Ailsa's own plans for the future, which were roundly approved. Then it was time for her to retire to bed. She could hardly keep her eyes open. The huge meal and the two ciders hadn't helped.

'Can you come to our First Day of Spring party on the 21st?' Flora asked her as they made their way towards the door.

'That's only a few days away.'

'Yes, Saturday, 12:00 noon. It's at Gallipot Cottage. We want everyone's presence there to bless the wildflower meadow and make it plentiful for the coming year.'

'I'll definitely try.' Ailsa knew she would have a thousand and one things to do at her new place and couldn't spare the time.

'Please do,' said Flora, taking both Ailsa's hands in hers. 'I think we share a bond.'

Ailsa looked into the pale grey eyes staring into hers so openly and could almost believe her.

'Alright. I'll be there.'

Half an hour later, Philippa popped her head around the bedroom door. Ailsa was reading, having gone from desperately tired to wide awake as soon as she climbed into bed.

'I've brought you a hot chocolate,' said her aunt, popping it down on the bedside table. She gave Ailsa a kiss on her forehead, which made her feel like a six-year-old again, not an unpleasant experience, and then she went out of the door. Before it closed, her head appeared again.

'And I didn't tell you about the baby,' she said to her niece, her eyebrows lifting.

'Well. I must have heard it somewhere,' Ailsa replied.

'Mmm?' and Philippa left her to her uneasy dreams.

Chapter 3

Pulling on the roadside in front of Nightowl's Hide, as her new driveway was littered with work vans, Ailsa was pleased to see that the emailed photos from the builders didn't do it justice from the outside. It looked finished and very attractive.

From the front, it had mellow stone walls with a long sloping roof, which had two dormer windows set into it. The two downstairs windows had stone lintels and the central door was enclosed by a porch, which she fully intended would have roses growing around it next year. Why have a country cottage and not have roses around the door? There was a chimney at each gable end and it looked perfectly in keeping with the rest of the small village. Not even Mrs. Pennyquick could complain.

From the inside, it could be a very different story, judging by the drilling and hammering going on. She had been assured that her bedroom and bathroom were finished and that all workable parts of the kitchen were already fitted. She then pulled into her small, private driveway to the right of the cottage. Pushing the side door, she stepped straight into a light, bright and modern kitchen.

The window to the right of the door gave more light over the sink. A brand new range oven was next to it, further down to her right. A large bifold door brought even more light into the kitchen at the far end. She was pleased to see that there was plenty of room for a table in front of the bifolds, perfect for a coffee as she gazed onto her land.

There was a noise ahead from a white painted door as it opened. Ade, her main communicator, poked his head through.

'Thought I'd heard something. Now then,' he said, stepping into the kitchen from the small utility room, 'what do you think to it?'

Ailsa looked around. The kitchen looked finished to her, apart from a bit of tiling over one of the worktops.

'I have to say I'm really pleased with it. It looks better and more finished than I hoped.'

He grinned widely, then stopped.

'You might not be saying that when you see the two spare bedrooms. Only halfway through plastering them yet, so there'll be quite a bit of dust.'

He looked apologetic.

'I expected that. You kept me informed and it was my choice to move here before it was completely finished. The new owners of my flat wanted to be in today, so there was no point in hanging about.'

'You have a wander round love and see what you think. Shall I take your bag into your bedroom?'

'It's okay. There are only clothes and a few books in. The people who bought the flat also wanted to buy the furniture there, which I was pleased about, as it wouldn't have looked right here. I've just got a few boxes of things in the boot, which can wait for now.'

'Does that mean you haven't got a bed to sleep in?' He looked aghast.

'It's being delivered tomorrow. I thought I'd just sleep on the floor tonight.'

He looked doubly aghast until Ailsa started chuckling.

'I've booked a room at the Falcon Inn next door for tonight. I could have stayed another night at my aunt's but–' she shrugged.

'I've got aunts like that.' Ade nodded wisely.

'Don't get me wrong. She's lovely. It's just very intense there.'

'Where's that then?'

'Farstone.'

Ade lifted his eyebrows in recognition.

'And I can do without all that witchy stuff at the moment.'

He scratched his head.

'Let me get this right. You don't want to be involved in witchy stuff, so you move to a witch's cottage in another witchy village?' he asked incredulously.

Ailsa burst out laughing.

'In a nutshell, yes. Is this another witchy village then?'

She hadn't realised that it had a reputation apart from Nightowl's Hide itself.

'Well, I believe there were one or two around here. If not here, then close by. You're better off talking to Sylvia Pennyquick about it. She used to be a history teacher before she retired last year and she knows all about the local history. Married to the vicar.'

This was news to Ailsa; Mrs. P. hadn't mentioned her husband.

'Yes, I've already been in contact with Mrs. Pennyquick who gave me more instructions on what I could and couldn't do with the house than the area planning committee did'

Aid chuckled.

'Yes, she's a bit bossy. Still talks to you like she's a teacher. Her heart's in the right place, though, and she's passionate about Hatton-le-Hollow.'

'I can tell,' Ailsa said, pulling a face.

*

After a quick tour of the place and finding that the plasterers *were* making a lot of dust, and the electrics were still being finished off in the sitting room, along with the skirting boards being fitted under the window, she grabbed her bag and headed next door to The Falcon.

As she made for the pub's main entrance, a man unfolded himself from one of the benches outside. He was tall, very tall, with strange reflective amber eyes that caught her attention even more than his height. His hair was very dark with lighter brown streaks in it and was resting on his shoulders. He had a very exotic look to him and she couldn't help noticing that he was possibly the best-looking man she had ever seen.

While making these observations, she had almost slowed to a halt and, feeling embarrassed, put her head down and started walking again. She was brought up suddenly by the sight of a wolf emerging from behind the vacated bench.

She gave an involuntary gasp and her whole body stiffened as she stared at the creature. It came up to her with a smooth, loping stride - much like that of its master - and started sniffing at her while she remained rooted to the spot. She cursed the man for not calling the animal off, whilst still keeping all her attention focused on the wolf.

Slowly, after seeming to make its mind up, it lowered its head - and licked her hand, wagging its tail as it did so. The man caught her eye and gave the ghost of a smile, a hint of mischief in those distinctive eyes. Then he gave her the briefest of nods before he and the wolf both walked off down the road.

Ailsa started to breathe normally again and rushed into the pub.

'Is that a wolf?' he said by way of introduction. The landlord looked up from polishing the glasses.

'I'm sorry, I'm Ailsa McKendry. I'm staying here tonight. Was it a wolf?'

The words came tumbling out at super speed.

'Conall's wolf, I expect you mean?'

'So it *is* a wolf?'

'No, it's called Wolf, that's its name. It's a–' he turned to an elderly man sitting at the bar. 'What type's that dog of Conall's?'

'Search me. Oh, hang on, Finnish something or other. Laphound maybe?'

'Well, it looks like a wolf to me,' Ailsa grumbled, annoyed with herself. She loved all animals, but this one had terrified her for a moment.

'It looks like a wolf to everybody. Most people around here know Wolf well and know that he's got a gentle nature, but visitors and newcomers...' he said, pointing at Ailsa, 'don't know this and are rightly terrified. I've had to ask him not to bring him in here at busy times of the year.'

So, gentle nature, eh? Ailsa thought that this Conall had enjoyed the encounter just a bit too much. She glowered, making the landlord pull back a few inches.

'I expect you'd like to see where you're staying?'

Belatedly, she remembered her manners.

'I'm sorry. Yes, please, that would be lovely.'

She was staying in one of three small self-contained rooms built behind the pub.

'And can I say?' the landlord added, 'Welcome to the village. I hear you're our new neighbour.'

She thanked him and then followed him through, glad that the locals seemed friendly, even if certain people and their wolf dogs were a little more unnerving.

Chapter 4

'I don't believe it.'

'I'm sorry, Miss McKendry. They promised it would be today, but one of their drivers has been off sick so they're a bit stretched.'

'Couldn't your supplier deliver my bed straight to me instead of you?'

'More than my life's worth to ask them. Besides, there's a large van full of furniture. I can't ask them to make a special trip. If they did that for everyone...'

'Yes, I see, I see, ' Ailsa spat impatiently and then took a deep breath. It wasn't the poor man's fault. 'There's no problem. It's only one more day. Thank you for letting me know.'

There was a moment's silence at the other end of the phone. He was probably crossing himself in thanks.

'Oh, that's good,' he breathed, 'I promise it will be with you by mid-afternoon tomorrow.'

She put her phone back in her pocket. It wasn't as if she couldn't afford another night here at The Falcon. She was a popular singer on the Folk circuit. She had even appeared in the charts a couple of times with folk-rock songs she had composed herself. She did enjoy writing that type of song, but she was a folk purist at heart, singing the same songs that had been heard in this country since medieval times. Everyone knew 'Sumer is icumen in', and that was a Folk round from the 1200s.

The hits brought in a substantial amount with the albums providing regular income from royalties, but most of her money had been earned from touring the Folk festivals and mainstream music festivals from Easter through to All Hallows - and then to the Winter Solstice. That was her main source of income, and what she had saved had enabled her to renovate this cottage, with money left over for her dream. This was why she had needed the land.

The fact that it was in a strip that went so far back was such a bonus. If she held the Folk

31

festivals, she had in mind they would be towards the back of the land. They were only going to be relatively small affairs, Gatherings sounded more appropriate. They would be out of earshot from any of the houses in Hatton-le-Hollow, which were mostly set along the Main Street anyway- and over the Green at the other side of the road, well away from her.

This meant that there would be no objections to noise, even though Folk music was definitely one of the least noisy of the musical genres. It also meant that any cars could be parked well out of the way. She intended to make a nice-sized garden for herself, she needed somewhere to relax. Then she'd use the other acreage for, firstly, a car park behind the tall garden wall she was having built. Then an area where she hoped tents could be pitched, then the performing area, before you reached the old round barn.

The round barn itself she would use, once rethatched, as an area to sit, and to eat and drink. She would be selling mead, cider and ale if she could get a temporary licence and would invite the local bakery and cafe to have a stall there. She could also direct others to The Falcon for a hot meal. Stan, the landlord's, rooms would also be full, so he had been very happy about the boost in trade. She'd had a word with him months ago.

The best thing was she had already got a TEN – a Temporary Events Notice for the Summer Solstice in June. She only wanted a small Folk festival three, maybe four times a year. She was thinking May Day, which she would miss this year as the land wouldn't be ready. Then Summer Solstice, which she was hoping would be the first this year. Then Lammas, or Lughnasadh, hopefully on the first day of August.

She had semi-retired at the grand old age of thirty-five, as she had found the touring of festival venues, especially in the colder months, exhausting. She was pinning all her hopes on these events on her own land. She would still attend a few of the other places she was used to visiting, that didn't clash with hers, but she intended to slow down before she burnt herself out, so would cut most of the large venues out.

This decision had been hastened by her band breaking up. Ashwood were all quite a bit older than her. They had been on the folk music scene well before she had arrived and were nearing retirement age - and in a couple of cases well past it. A musician, of course, never retired. Music was in their blood, but they all, to a man, wanted to slow down. So amicably, they had agreed to part company.

One of them, the drummer, was retiring permanently as he was in his late seventies. Another, the flautist, was going to live in France. They had all agreed to reunite for Ailsa's own festivals and for a couple of their favourite festivals. The smaller ones, the type Ailsa was aiming for herself, where everyone seemed to know everybody else. She now had to decide whether she wanted to go solo or find another band. Solo didn't appeal. The camaraderie between her and the band would be sorely missed.

Leaving the bag she had packed to take home, she made her way through the back door of the pub to have a word with Stan. He was frying some bacon.

'Do you want a bacon sandwich?'

'Oh, I didn't realise breakfast was included.'

'It isn't, but you look like you're in need of one.'

She didn't think she was that skinny. She was naturally slim. That's all.

'You look worried,' he explained.

'Yes, my bed isn't arriving until tomorrow now so I was hoping that I could have the room for another night.'

Stan's face fell.

'I would Ailsa, but it's already rented out for the next couple of days. The other rooms are too.

34

It's a family get-together.' He handed her the bacon sandwich by way of apology.

'Oh damn. No worries. I'll just throw some blankets on the floor and I have new bedding and pillows in the car.'

'I've got spare blankets you can borrow?'

He was eager to make amends, although it was hardly his fault.

'I might take you up on that. I'll take my bag next door in a minute anyway and see what I need.'

'Coffee?' he asked.

'Please. Strong.'

'I thought you didn't want it strong yesterday?'

'I do today.'

She supposed she was just in a hurry to move in. She laughed to herself, remembering her reaction when she first saw Nightowl's Hide. Now it seemed like the home she'd never had. She felt an affinity with it and especially with the land. She couldn't wait until the workmen were out and she could move in permanently.

Chapter 5

After dropping her bag off in her bedroom, she looked out of the window and down onto the land. She could see almost all of it. There were trees around the edges that broke into it, stopping it from being a completely open area of land, but it looked all the better for it.

Ailsa studied it as she sat on the window seat. She could see the area where she hoped the tents would be pitched. The trees provided little oases of separation, which would also protect from strong winds. Just after the camping area were two square hedged areas, one on either side, yet not opposite each other. The right-side hedged area was set about forty feet further down. She thought that in the future, this is where she might put two shepherd's huts, in each of the partial enclosures, as they would be very private. Past all that was the potential stage area. Just one stage so that everyone saw each act and didn't miss anything by wandering around different sets. Of course, wandering around itself would be encouraged as she would have a few locals with stalls selling homemade food and handmade goods, plus the food and drink in the round barn during intervals.

Bands or individuals could hold impromptu acoustic performances around the festival area, and she hoped in the unhappy but likely event of bad weather that there would be room in the round barn for everyone to cram in. It was huge, so she had high expectations.

Thinking about the barn, the thatchers had been to give an estimate. It was going to be expensive, but it was a skilled job. She knew the price was the norm and possibly quite a bit cheaper than some. She didn't mind so much as they had promised they could start in a day or two, by which time the cottage should be finished.

They also knew someone who could renew the wattle and daub underneath the beams and thatch. The walls themselves weren't very high, as most of the height came from the massive conical-shaped thatched roof itself.

She listened to the noises downstairs, thankful that they were far fewer than yesterday. The other bedrooms had been plastered and were drying out. She could feel that the battle was almost won. Heading downstairs to have a quick word with

Ade, she then went out onto the driveway to fetch the bedding out of the car.

This driveway that she'd had made and gravelled at the right-hand side of the cottage was her own personal driveway, whereas the other wider one to the left, next to The Falcon's driveway, was the one for festival goers leading to the car park. At the moment, there were a few work vans in it and next week, the thatchers would use it to get to the barn.

Before she could reach the car door, a round, ruddy and smiling face appeared over the fence of the cottage next door.

'Hello, you're my new neighbour. I know who you are and I love your music. I'm thrilled to have you living next door. It's brilliant!'

'Oh hello! You're Miss Bright?'

They had only communicated through the solicitors. Ailsa was very grateful that she seemed happy enough about the noise, renovation and plans.

'That's right. Please call me Star.'

There was a moment's pause. Ailsa dug her nails into her palm so that she didn't laugh and lose any goodwill she had already built up. Star Bright? Really? She daren't ask if it was a nickname in case it wasn't and the poor girl just had particularly cruel parents.

'Star' she gulped. 'Very nice to meet you.'

A drill started up from somewhere in the cottage.

'Oh' said Star 'you're still in the middle of it, I see. Come over for a cup of tea and we can get to know each other. You'll have to go around the fence, I'm afraid, but maybe we could think about putting a gate in the fence...'

And with that bombshell, she vanished from whatever she'd been standing on, leaving Ailsa with no option but to go around the fence unless she wanted to appear rude. One thing was for sure. There would definitely, *definitely*, be no gate.

As she walked up to the cottage, she could see a wide paved pathway at the side and a lawned strip of land next to the fence. On the grass stood a bright pink, upturned box. The fence was six feet high and Star had obviously been keeping an eye on proceedings. Oh dear. Ailsa was sociable as far as it went, but she did like her privacy. She hoped the girl wasn't going to be a problem.

She knocked on the open door and received a very cheery 'Come right in, make yourself at home.' Star had a chubby, homely body that matched her chubby, homely face.

'I have chamomile, mint, strawberry and lavender.'

Ailsa thought she was talking about the produce in her garden until she held a teapot up.

'I don't suppose you've got any ordinary tea, have you?'

Star looked disappointed but reached into the cupboard.

'Earl Grey?' she asked.

'Perfect, thank you.'

Ailsa looked around the kitchen. The room was small but still had space for a table and two chairs at the end, looking out over the garden. There were pink voile curtains pulled back at the sides of the windows. Peering closely, she could see that there were silver stars on them. Hanging from the ceiling on lengths of thin ribbon were a variety of flimsy objects: stars, crescent moons, suns, but mostly stars of gold, silver and pink. There seemed to be a theme going on. Stars, yes, but also pink, thought Ailsa.

Star indicated a chair painted in a particularly lurid pink. Ailsa had to avoid the dangly objects, being quite tall, whereas Star forged a path underneath them, being just over five feet by Ailsa's estimations.

Ailsa reached the table and noticed that the unoccupied chair was actually occupied. A large, fluffy marmalade cat was looking at Ailsa the same way as her headmistress used to when she'd done something wrong again. Ailsa frowned.

'Your cat doesn't want to move. It's giving me murderous looks' explained Ailsa.

'Charm! Get down.'

Star tried to shoo her off, but she wouldn't be shooed.

'You take my chair,' she said and then picked the cat up with an effort and plonked it on her knee, where it continued to stare across the table at Ailsa, who hadn't realised cats could frown before.

'She's so spoilt 'laughed Star. 'She thinks she owns this cottage,' and Ailsa wasn't sure the cat was wrong in that thought.

'I'm surprised you don't drink herbal teas, considering who your cousin is, ' Star went on.'

'Mary?' Ailsa was puzzled.

'Flora Gardwicke?' Star was also puzzled.

'Flora? My cousin?'

Star nodded, satisfied as she had taken this as confirmation instead of the incredulous query it was.

'No. I mean, Flora's not my cousin.'

'Isn't she?' and then a smile. 'Are you sure? Because Sylvia told me she was.'

'Who does this fount of all wisdom think she is?' Ailsa could feel her hackles rising.

This village of Hatton was as bad as Farstone for people knowing everyone else's business.

'She's an ex-teacher. She knows all about this area.'

'She may well do, but she can leave me out of her gossip'

Ailsa folded her arms and frowned in a parody of the cat, whose paws were probably folded too, under the folds of fur.

Star looked taken aback.

'She used to teach me at secondary school' Star's big eyes were suspiciously shiny. Oh, please, thought Ailsa, don't start with the tears - and then immediately felt bad. Star was the type who thought everyone was wonderful and couldn't understand why other people didn't.

'I'm sorry,' she said quickly. 'I've just come across her before, just after I bought next door. She made me agree to umpteen things before I passed her inspection, including keeping the owl in the garden.'

'Lilith!' Star said excitedly. 'You've seen her then?'

'Yes,' she replied uncertainly, 'it's a fixture on my land.'

'Yes, especially around the barn. I hope she will always stay around here.'

Ailsa's eyebrows knitted together. The girl - and she couldn't have been much more than twenty years old -seemed nice and friendly, but mostly daffy, and she wasn't sure she could take much more at the moment. She was very perplexing.

'Well, thank you for the tea. Nice to meet you. You too, Charm.' Ailsa said this last through gritted teeth and returned the death stare she received. 'I'd better be getting back next door.'

'Your bed hasn't arrived, has it?' Ailsa whipped her head up. 'So if you wanted to stay here, I have a lovely spare bedroom.'

She'd kill Ade for not keeping his mouth shut.

'It's okay. I have something to sleep on and I was just fetching my bedding out of the car when I saw you.'

The girl looked disappointed.

'I thought it would be a good chance to get to know each other. Are you sure?'

'Absolutely, but thank you for your kind offer, Star.' The big brown eyes looked at her. It was like facing a Labrador puppy. 'and I'm sure we'll see each other lots.'

Ailsa realised that, unfortunately, this was inevitable. Giving her new neighbour a cheery wave, she walked quickly around to her car. As she carried the bedding in, she saw Ade at the door.

'You're not sleeping here tonight without a bed, are you?'

'Yes,' she sighed.

'Wouldn't advise it. It's going to be a cold one,' he muttered, looking up at the sky.

'I'll turn the heating up,' she responded.

'Ah, as to that. Boiler engineer's been and tested it all. Turned it high, then turned it off. Then he's coming back in the morning to turn it on again. He wants to check it then and told us not to turn it back on again today.'

Ailsa's eyes looked up to the heavens, which seemed to be conspiring against her today.

'That's no problem' came a gleeful voice from over the fence. The clatter of the pink box preceded the happy face peeping over at them. 'She can stay here, can't you, Ailsa?'

There was a short silence while Ailsa desperately tried to think of an excuse, but none came to mind.

'Yes, I suppose I can. Thank you, Star.'

Chapter 6

After telling Star that she had a few things to sort out, Ailsa escaped into Nightowl's Hide. The noise and even the cold didn't seem quite so bad now.

When had she become so antisocial? The poor girl was friendly, neighbourly and possibly quite lonely and all she could think of was trying to avoid her. There was no avoiding her tonight, though.

She would have to make the best of it. Let someone inside the hard shell she had built around herself. She had only perhaps in the last five years seen how much of this was due to her mother. For some reason, still undisclosed, she had poisoned Ailsa's mind against Farstone and all the place stood for.

When she had visited with her dad and stayed with his sister at the inn, she had enjoyed it but later at home, there were terrible arguments between her parents. She had realised a long time ago that her father had left the village of his birth purely for a quiet life. It was obvious he wasn't going to get one if they stayed there. All to no avail because as soon as she was seventeen and due to go to university, they split up, which didn't have the devastating impact on Ailsa that it should have.

Her mother had never forgiven her father for taking her back to Farstone after they married. She had never fitted in. When Peggy had to deliver Ailsa in an emergency home birth, her mother had been inconsolable, saying that Ailsa was now cursed like the rest of the village. She remembered this vividly as her mother had announced it loudly and drunkenly years later at the annual Peverel Hall fete. All she could remember were at least fifty pairs of eyes on her seven-year-old self before Philippa came and picked her up, taking her back to the inn. Her mother had never forgiven Peggy, even though she had probably saved her life and Ailsa's too. Happy days, she thought ironically.

It was no wonder she liked to keep herself to herself, except for tonight, of course, when Star had promised to make her something special for dinner. She would take a bottle of wine, it might make everything seem better.

She went from room to room checking her new place out. She smiled to herself. The furniture she had ordered was arriving on Monday and would really make this place seem like home. She had chosen the basics, the most essential being two Chesterfield sofas in a pale tan leather. They looked vintage enough to fit in with the old character interior she had gone for, but would be her own to wear in herself.

The other bits and pieces, she was looking forward to shopping for in Pickering, to give it the proper old cottage ambience she was looking for. She hoped she would do credit to Effie Scritchell. Perhaps being turned into a well-loved home would erase any unhappy memories of when she lived there in poverty, and replace them with feelings of contentment and peace for her spirit.

The wood burner was in place, but only having had central heating before, she would have to ask Ade how to use it tomorrow. She was such a city girl now, but was looking forward to her return to the country life, strangely enough. She shivered. It *was* cold in here now that the heating was off. Colder than it was outside.

Ade thought it had needed a new part that the engineer had found to be faulty, so she couldn't complain about it from a safety point of view. He was doing his job well, even if Ade was annoyed as he was hoping for a low even temperature to dry the plaster out.

She went back through to the kitchen and looked through the bifold doors down the land. No fences or walls separated what would be her garden from the other acreage yet. She could see a white object against the dark hedge at the right of her garden. The small white stone figure of the owl. Lilith, Star had called it. She wandered down towards it after opening the bifold doors a little so there was no possibility of disturbing Star and her pink crate.

On reaching it, she examined it properly for the first time. There was no name carved there of either the owl or the sculptor. It was a primitive imagining of a large barn owl and difficult to date. It could easily have been carved by a modernist, avant-garde sculptor or a contemporary of Effie's. It was representative and therefore timeless, but there was no doubt that this was a magnificently regal owl. She felt almost cowed in its presence, a little bit like she had been with the redoubtable Charm, the cat.

It was strange as she normally got on great with animals. They just took to her for some reason and she felt comfortable in their presence. Charm, or perhaps Charm(less) was a better name, seemed to be weighing her up and she wasn't sure she had come out of it particularly well.

She put out her hand and stroked at the top of the made-to-scale owl figure in front of her, which was placed on top of a stone plinth. She suddenly had a wonderful feeling of calm as she looked into the wide-open eyes. They scarily reminded her of Star's eyes earlier. Smiling, she stroked Lilith's head again..

'I promise that you will stay here as long as I live here. I can see that you belong here.'

She quickly realised she was basically talking to herself, took her hand from the owl's head and looked towards the house in case anyone had seen her. Smiling again, she turned to go back to the cottage when a flutter of wings made her jump. She turned back to look up the land but couldn't see anything. She unaccountably looked at the stone figure behind her, which was still as lifeless as it had been and then laughed at herself. This place was starting to affect her.

*

There was still a good hour or so until she had to present herself for the special dinner at Star's, so she strolled down to the shop at the entrance of the village. At least this place was easy to get to, unlike Farstone. There were quite a few villages skirting the edge of Farstone Moor. There was Farstone itself, of course, a place almost inaccessible in times gone by. It still had a hairy z-bend, single

49

track, almost vertical road leading to it even now. She always gritted her teeth every time she had to drive down it - and back up again, as it was the only way in or out.

Hatton-le-Hollow, usually known as Hatton to the locals, led out onto the moors just the same, but the road in was much easier in comparison. The village itself nestled in a hollow, as the name suggested, which protected it from most of the bad weather which affected the great expanse of moor. It seemed like this part of Yorkshire was made up of nothing but moor with verdant, nestling villages dotted here and there. You had to go many miles to reach the nearest market town of Pickering for civilisation, or Helmsley on the other side, with the nearest city being York.

On reaching the shop, she went inside and introduced herself. The country ways were getting to her. At any other time, she would have just asked for what she wanted and got out. She carried the bottle of rose wine, the safest option, in her hand as there were no plastic carriers. The man behind the counter had looked aghast when she'd asked. Now, she was advertising the bottle to anyone who saw her and cared to make a judgement. A canvas non-see-through bag for the next time, she promised herself silently.

She looked up to see two figures further out on the edge of the moor. They were in an intense conversation. She could tell by the dog that one of the men was Conall. His companion looked towards her, but she couldn't see his face for the hood almost covering it.

A voice came from the other side of her. Two people had crept up on her unnoticed.

'Hello, my dear. Forgive me, but are you the lady who has moved into Nightowl's Hide?'

She took in the spectacles, the thinning hair, the benevolent expression - but mostly she took in the dog collar and realised that this was Mrs. Pennyquick's husband, vicar of this parish. Was this woman by his side, the redoubtable Sylvia Pennyquick, then? She was a lot younger than Ailsa had imagined her to be.

'I am. Pleased to meet you, Reverend Pennyquick.'

She held out the hand that wasn't carrying the bottle, which she was trying to hide behind her back.

'Welcome to our village. Miss Reed.'

Miss Reed?

'I think you'll find us very friendly here. I hope we'll see you at our church, such a friendly community.'

Ailsa was an atheist.

'I - possibly not. I'm - I'm not really- although I do believe the churches are definitely an important part of a small community like this. It's just that....and I expect this is your wife, Sylvia? We've corresponded,' she floundered and held her hand out to her.

Both the vicar and the woman looked confused, then he laughed.

'Oh goodness me no, this is my niece, Esme Pennyquick, my late brother's daughter. She's like a daughter to us, too.'

He smiled across at her and she grabbed his arm and squeezed it.

'Hi,' she eventually held her hand out to Ailsa. 'It's so nice to meet you. I love your music. Even if you don't get to the church…' she grinned at Ailsa with undisguised amusement. 'And I hope you'll visit my cafe down the road from your place?'

'I'm absolutely sure I will replied Ailsa, then remembered. 'I'd actually like a word with you about catering.'

'You've heard about her bakery, then? Best pastry you've ever tasted.' The reverend smiled.

'I haven't, but I will be in to try it now.'

'Please do call into the vicarage as well, we will be very pleased to see you.'

I'm not sure Sylvia will though, thought Ailsa as they said their goodbyes.

She brought the bottle from behind her back where she'd been trying to hide it, just in time to cross paths with Conall. His long-legged strides had soon brought him in front of her. She was struck dumb once more. His charisma was enough to draw you in. It made you feel like you were in the presence of some form of royalty, some higher being, and if she could have moved from the spot, she would probably have knelt on the floor before him so he could lay his foot on her back to subjugate her.

She tried to snap out of it, but she was suddenly met with his amber eyes catching the light ethereally, as he looked at her own blue eyes. She felt drawn to him as you would be drawn to the sight of the sea crashing below a cliff. It was dangerous. It was a feeling that meant she was out of control, and she didn't like it.

She set her facial expression to 'pompous' and started to cross the road, but a moment later, she felt hot breath on her hand, and Wolf's head came forward to lick her fingers. He looked up at her expectantly, so she tentatively stroked his head and neck. He looked very happy and leant against her legs. If this was a wolf, it was an extremely friendly one.

'You're a big softie, aren't you?' Wolf seemed to agree as he nudged her arm, wanting another fuss made of him. She duly obliged.

She looked up to see that same faintly amused expression on Conall's face, that same half smile on his sensual lips. My God, he was the most gorgeous man she had ever seen. Everything about him. His slim but muscly physique and his classically chiselled facial features. The way he moved like a dancer - like an animal. His clothes fitting tightly across his chest, his arms, his legs...

She came to, as though out of a dream. She drew back. She felt like she had been drawn in, fascinated by a snake holding its prey. She rushed past him and just caught that half smile again. Was he mocking her? There was one thing for sure: it had made her crave normality. The fact that she was looking forward to Star to provide this normality, showed how much this being out of control had worried her.

Chapter 7

There were unidentifiable smells coming from the kitchen as Star opened the door. Ailsa's olfactory senses didn't quite know what to make of them.

'Mmm, something smells good', she said diplomatically whilst crossing the fingers of one hand behind her back and handing the bottle of wine over with the other.

'Oh, sorry, I don't drink alcohol. You take it home with you. I've got some homemade non-alcoholic drinks here for us.'

Ailsa didn't drink a lot of wine either, but she looked at the bottle longingly. She was relying on a couple of glasses to get her through the evening, and the meal too, by the smell of it. Star had changed her jumper and was now wearing a red and black spotted top, which clashed horribly with her red frizzy hair, although possibly the pink walls clashed even more.

'Let me show you to your room and then we can have a nice cup of tea.'

Herbal tea, Ailsa remembered.

'Or we could go straight on to the homemade juice?'

'That sounds good', Ailsa answered, thinking that it would be the lesser of two evils. Star led her through into a small hallway painted in a mauve emulsion, with the same sort of things pinned on the wall there as were hanging in the kitchen. Star held the door of the living room open so Ailsa could peep in. It was pink on two walls, one of which was thankfully, mostly broken up by a large window looking out onto the main street.

The other two walls were mauve again, in place for a long time, possibly from the late '60s/ early '70s psychedelic period by the look of things. The steep wooden stairs led up to a tiny landing and to the back, over the kitchen, was the largest bedroom.

'This is mine, so I can see the garden last thing at night - and Lilith.' Star smiled.

She could see Ailsa's garden from here, too.

'I really hope it's not going to disturb you with me having the festivals a few times a year?'

'No, not at all,' Star squealed. 'I'm looking forward to it and I'll be there.'

The open, innocent and happy smile melted Ailsa's unsociable heart. She must stop giving this good soul a hard time, even if the hard time was only in Ailsa's mind.

'I appreciate that,' she said and meant it.

Star's bedroom had been predictably pink and full of all paraphernalia. Astrological symbols vied with occult symbols, from pentagrams to black cats. Ailsa glanced down the stairs to find Charm(less) lodged on the bottom step, staring up at her - frowning. She looked away quickly.

'And this is your room.'

The smaller bedroom on the other side of the landing was devoid of any other objects except the normal bed, lamps, bedside cabinets and chest of drawers. Of course, the walls were mauve, which was to be expected. She was convinced there had been a special offer of 75% off from the nearest hardware store, as no one else would want this shade. There was also a patchwork quilt of mismatched colours. Disturbingly, Ailsa found she liked this.

The bathroom was next. This seemed pleasantly normal with white walls and the bare minimum of accoutrements. She was thrown for a moment until she put her head around the door to see the toilet seat had a psychedelic swirly pattern of pink, purple, yellow and green on it. She backed out quickly.

'So now you know where everything is, we can go downstairs and eat and you can tell me everything about yourself.'

Ailsa groaned inwardly. For a private person, that was possibly the scariest set of words you could put together. People couldn't understand that even if you appeared on stage before hundreds and more often, thousands of people, you could still feel like your own company much of the time and also like your private life to stay private.

*

They were sitting on the two chairs at the table. Charm(less) had vacated the other chair in favour of the cushion in front of the open fire. They were on their second glass of the most unholy concoction of dandelion, tarragon, apple juice and honey. With the addition of the honey, Ailsa had high hopes it would taste like a non-alcoholic mead, but the bitterness was still there, only thinly disguised by the sweetness.

She finished the glass and unfortunately, Star filled it up again despite her protests. Star had been buoyed by Ailsa's completely false appreciation of it. That's what you get for lying through your teeth, thought Ailsa, although she couldn't look into Star's wide, innocent eyes and tell her it was foul.

She vaguely wondered to herself at what stage she had become tactful and lost the sarcasm. She wasn't, at this moment, sure that tactful was a good thing to be. She took another sip, it seemed to be growing on her.

Star came across to the table with a huge steaming crockpot. She put it down on a stone slab in the middle of the table and removed the lid. It looks delicious. If she was surprised at that, she was less surprised that the smell was still off-putting.

'It looks lovely, Star,' she said truthfully, 'What is it?'

'It's a casserole of my own devising. All things from my – ' she faltered 'from the garden, vegetables and herbs mostly, as I don't eat meat.'

This was fine with Ailsa, as although she didn't exactly count herself as a vegetarian, she didn't eat a lot of meat either.

'So,' Star continued, 'there's carrots. turnip, cabbage, broccoli, sprouts…'

Sprouts?

'Onion peas, beans'- Star went on. She seemed to have thrown every vegetable known to man at it. Ailsa could see little bits of meat on the surface. She frowned.

'Is that meat?'

Star peered at the dish. Ailsa had learnt that she wore glasses normally, which explained the wide-eyed look. She felt like suggesting she wear them all the time. If only to recognise the pinkness of the place as perhaps something she should address.

'Oh no,' Star laughed, 'that's mackerel, in tomato sauce, tinned.'

Ailsa looked at her.

'There's also honey, my homemade chutney and some parmesan cheese in it,' Star smiled.

Ailsa kept looking at her, with her newly found tact rapidly disappearing.

'Oh, and a couple of sliced bananas.'

There was a pregnant pause.

'Super! I love a banana and mackerel in tomato sauce casserole' said Ailsa, the sarcasm returning to full force.

'Oh, good. I hope you would.'

She hoped she would?

Ailsa blew on it to cool it, picked up a spoon, put it down to check her phone, drank the rest of the dandelion juice, then, having no more excuses, put a spoonful to her lips- and mentally preparing herself, swallowed it. No, it was no good. After hoping for a miracle, she realised it tasted as disgusting as it sounded. Some recipes created at random with seemingly odd ingredients turned out to be triumphs of culinary achievement. This wasn't one of them.

She arranged her features into something resembling appreciation.

'Lovely. The casserole. Lovely. Thank you, Star.'

She was just debating whether to fake an emergency phone call from Philippa when Star rushed around the table to give her a hug.

'I *knew* you'd like it,' she said, like she'd won the lottery. Ailsa, caught wrong-footed, kept quiet and ate the rest of the bowlful, washing it down with the equally unpalatable dandelion juice. It was going to be a long night.

*

Ailsa rolled off the settee with an elegance usually attributed to Rudolph Nureyev. Charm(less) eyed her hostilely as she landed next to her on the fluffy white rug.

'Oh hello, you... you... Cat.' Ailsa said, attempting to look Charm in the eye. Charm looked away in disgust. Ailsa laughed uproariously, in direct contrast to how funny the situation actually was.

Star was already rolling around on the floor, having fallen from her chair five minutes before.

She was lying on her back, cackling, like a rotund ladybird that couldn't right itself.

Ailsa guided herself slowly back up to the sofa, dislodging the many throws strewn across it to disguise its shabbiness.

'So you're doing a course to learn how to be a green witch?' Ailsa asked this quite normally as though it were an everyday thing.

Yes, loving it,' slurred Star. 'It's what I've always been without actually knowing it.'

Charm(less) planted herself on Ailsa's feet and Ailsa was so shocked that she let her. The full-on Death Stare was still there though. Maybe she was just holding her prisoner, her bulk holding Ailsa down so that there was no escape from Star Cottage.

'I don't like witches,' said Ailsa unequivocally and nodded sagely as she said it, causing her to feel even more dizzy.

'You're only saying that because you don't know about witches in the pert… the applic… the pertinental… The Proper Way.'

'I was brought up in a village of bloo… of blooming witches, don't forget. I don't care whether they were green, red, black or white.'

'You had an anti-witch upbringing.' Star eased herself back into her chair. Charm deigned to come and join her.

'I did' shouted Ailsa, wondering why her voice had gone up by five decibels, 'but there was a pre…a profita… a damn good reason. Ailsa wobbled over to the coffee table, where Star had placed another bottle of the horrible dandelion juice. It seemed to be tasting much better after the what? fifth? sixth? seventh glass? She poured herself another.

'Yes, your mother,' growled Star in a most un-Star-like manner,

'My mother? I suppose... Anyway, what do you know about my mother?'

Ailsa tipped the glass up and poured half the contents down her throat while the other half dribbled down her front.

'Everyone in Farstone knows about your mother. You poor so-, you poor soul. She was wicked.'

'Star! I think you have the wrong - the completely... Yes- idea,' managed Ailsa. Her mother had her problems, but she couldn't be called wicked, surely?

'Totally true. Promise Al- Ailsa.'

Another thing struck Ailsa, right between the eyes, before she went to sleep under the beady-eyed watchfulness of a disapproving marmalade cat.

'I thought you didn't drink alcohol?'

'I don't!' said Star in a petulant manner.

Ailsa tried to rearrange her features into a frown, befitting her thoughts, but burst out laughing instead.

'But… what have you put in this dang - dandelion juice? she managed.

'Only dandelion juice, apple juice, lots of sugar, honey and yeast. Left it for couple of months. Think? Can't drink that much. Anyway, twelve bottles left now' Star mumbled as her eyes were closing.

Ailsa's last thoughts before she fell into a deep sleep were - surely sugar and yeast - and time, produced alcohol? Then she fell into sweet oblivion punctuated by dreams of pink and purple bananas marching into a crockpot as mackerel swam by, chased by bottles of tomato sauce.

Chapter 8

It was well after midday when Ailsa had a rude awakening. A demonic shriek sounded from downstairs, making her sit bolt upright in bed, then collapse on the pillow again as internally, her head played the drum beat from Queen's We Will Rock You. Extremely loudly.

She managed to push herself upright and, without a visit to the bathroom, as the toilet seat would make her puke, she slowly went downstairs holding tightly onto the bannister. She couldn't even remember coming up to bed last night.

'Sorry,' whispered an apologetic Star who, if possible, looked even worse than Ailsa felt.

'I stood on Charm's tail.'

A smile crept onto Ailsa's lips. She turned towards Charm(less) and the cat turned towards her, eyes like slits. I swear, I absolutely swear, that cat knows exactly what I'm thinking, thought. Ailsa, unnerved.

'A-are you all right?' asked Star, who seemed quite content not to move from the kitchen table where a large glass of water sat in front of her.

'Three guesses.' Ailsa grabbed a glass and filled it up from the tap.

'I was just wondering... You know that dandelion juice we had?'

'I vaguely recall it, yes,'

Having drunk half a pint of water virtually in one go, she now gave Star a stare which rivalled that of the cat.

'Do you think there was something in it that made us ill?' went on Star.

Unbelievable!

'The something in it, Star, was all the ingredients that go to make very strong alcohol - and the illness is what's known in common parlance as one *hell* of a hangover.'

The look on Star's face made Ailsa regret her words, but really she needed to know that she had lethal weapons of mass destruction in her kitchen cupboards.

'But,–but, I'm a teetotaller. I've never drunk alcohol in my life!'

Ailsa sighed.

'Have you had much of your dandelion juice before?'

There was a pause.

'I have had a very small glass every night before I go to bed for the last two years.'

'Then you've been drinking alcohol for two years.'

'Oh no!' wailed Star. She looked genuinely distressed.

'Is it against your religion or something?'

'No, it's just that I can't stand the taste of it.' Perhaps next time leave the yeast out?' Ailsa smiled, taking pity on her.

'Now I'm going to thank you very much for your hospitality and the lovely–' she had to fight the urge to retch, 'casserole, but I'm going to head next door now to have another little nap.'

'Yes, I think I'll go back upstairs too as soon as I've' Star was also fighting the urge to retch, 'fed Charm.'

'I'm sure Charm could live off her fat for a few more hours until you feel better.'

She felt, rather than saw, the cat's malevolent gaze turn towards her. She ignored it. With a few more words of thanks from Ailsa and a barrage of 'sorrys' from Star, she finally made it back to Nightowl's Hide. She lay on half the duvet, on the carpet and pulled the other half over her - and she slept for another three hours.

*

Ailsa saw her reflection in the bathroom mirror. Her long, straw-coloured hair was sticking out at strange angles and her eyes, slightly pink like a rabbit's, were testament to the previous night's excesses.

She had made it to the kitchen to make a cup of tea, as her mouth still felt like a monkey had slept in it, when she heard the side gate go. The metal latch that closed the farmhouse gate across what would be the public driveway. One of the builders, perhaps? They had thankfully left her alone to sleep after Ade had assessed her situation at a glance. He said there were only two men left there finishing off and promised they would be as quiet as mice. In the event, a herd of buffalo could have rampaged through the place and she would have slept on.

She plodded outside and round to the far side in time to see Wolf walking towards her, accompanied by his master, who, of course, looked bloody gorgeous as he strode in her direction. The muscles in his legs stretching the tight suede trousers and.... Oh God. She looked down at herself wearing the same clothes as when he had seen her yesterday. The same clothes she had been wearing for 24 hours. She sniffed and a faint aroma of mackerel mixed with dandelion came up to meet her.

She just managed to smooth down her hair before he reached her. He grinned, which completely unnerved her.

'You look a little rough.'

'Just what a woman wants to be greeted with,' she was stung to reply.

'Your skin has a grey tinge,' and then he looked down at her clothes. He grinned again.

'So would yours if you'd spent the night drinking non-alcoholic juice with your neighbour.'

She was getting annoyed now. She knew she looked a mess and didn't need Conall to tell her this. An ironic laugh escaped from him.

'*Star's* non-alcoholic juice? You do know it is the very antithesis of non-alcoholic, don't you?'

'If I didn't before, I certainly do now. Wait a minute. If you knew it was alcoholic, why didn't you tell her? She really thought it was harmless juice.'

'She only had a very small glass sometimes, on a night, as far as I know, it wouldn't have done her any harm. You must be a bad influence on her.'

One eyebrow lifted in a very, to Ailsa's eyes, sensual manner.

'Well, I might not look as grey or rough - or even crumpled - if you had let her know.'

'Duly noted. I presume you have now let her know in no uncertain manner?'

'I have and if you're inferring I told her off, I didn't. At least I don't think I did. I was nice to her. I think?'

Ailsa was actually unsure.

'I don't think you can be anything else towards Star. She is one of the Earth's good creatures.'

A strange way to voice it, but yes, Ailsa had to agree. She looked up and caught his eye, and they smiled, which made her heart jump.

'Yes,' she said, 'a true innocent.'

For a few moments, nothing was said, then. Ailsa frowned.

'Did you want something?'

'The festivals, when are you holding them?'

'Oh, I was hoping to hold the first this year for the Summer Solstice. I will need the time beforehand to get everything ready etc. I have permission, if no objections are raised meantime, to hold the first festival over three days, two nights. I haven't heard back yet about the tent pitches. which I think are important. Before that though, I have to gravel the car park and cut the grass, maybe I'll hire some sheep 'lawnmowers' for next time. I have to make the outbuildings and sheds safe and finish thatching the round barn.'

'I'm glad you're rethatching it,' he nodded approvingly and she felt like she'd won first prize for good impressions.

'Yes, the thatchers have a good eco reputation.'

'What will you use it for?'

He spoke in a curiously old-fashioned way as though English wasn't his first language, yet he had no discernible accent. His voice was very calming, like waves of gentle positive energy sweeping over you. He was - unusual.

'I was hoping to use it as a seating area for people to eat there, possibly entertained by strolling players. I'm having locals, Esme, perhaps, to do the catering. For cooked lunches, they can pop next door to The Falcon.'

Another nod of approval, with the same effect on her.

'Would you–' The fresh air was making her feel more human, 'would you like to see it? The barn? I can show you what I plan to do.'

He smiled at her and they began to walk up the grounds together. He slowed his stride to hers and Wolf loped alongside his master. She suddenly realised.

'Why were you asking about the festivals?' she asked him.

'I am a musician. A strolling minstrel as you would have it,' he gave a gentle laugh, 'so I would be interested in playing here if you would have me?'

Like a shot, she thought before putting her baser instincts away and becoming the lady she had always thought she was.

'That would be marvellous. I was going to look into local musicians shortly, so you've saved me a job.'

'There are a few of us who live around here and we would be happy to play in Effie's garden.'

'You know of her?'

'Who doesn't, around here? A local legend, both her and Lilith.'

'What do you play?'

'The flute mostly. Tin whistle, wooden flutes, pan pipes, the shawm, a bombarde, which is an old bass wind instrument. You play the fiddle?'

'Yes, the electric fiddle on recordings and at large festivals, but for the smaller ones, I alternate between that and my beloved acoustic violin. What do your friends play?'

'The guitar and mandolin, the lyre harp, the bodhran... We often play together for our own pleasure or in establishments that will have us

72

there.' Again that strangely old-fashioned way of talking. 'We take it in turns to sing if we have to. I usually take a back seat as my mouth is otherwise occupied.'

Ailsa went off into a daydream and only realised she was touching her lips with her fingertips when Conall gave her a searching look. He went on.

'Your vocals,' he stopped and faced her, 'are surely unique. Heart-stopping. The upper range through to the lowest range has a versatility not achieved elsewhere, I believe.'

She looked at him in surprise, mixed with a little bit of disbelief. He *seemed* sincere and so did the smile he gave her now - and the reassuring touch on her arm, which told her of his honesty. A touch which made her insides turn to jelly.

'Well, thank you, kind sir,' she muttered, embarrassed. People had praised her voice many times before, God-given, sings like an angel, amazing vocal range, etc, etc., but this was the first time she had thought of it as true and not flattery. Her fault. She didn't think much of her talents. Was that her mother's fault again? Saying she would never make a career in music, or should she start accepting it was her own weakness, her own failing for being so easily influenced by a stronger personality than she was?

They had reached the round barn now. It still gave her the thrill she had felt on first seeing it. They went inside. The calm and peaceful feeling was also still there. She stood for a moment, her eyes closed, capturing the feeling inside her. She opened them to find him looking at her in an amused fashion.

'Yes, it has that effect, does it not?'

How does he know? He felt it too, perhaps?

There was a sudden noise. A flapping of wings. Wolf's ears pricked up. Conall pointed towards a high rafter in the far corner, underneath a part of the old thatch that still clung on. She followed his sightline and was shocked to see a large creature, like a ghost, gazing down on them.

'Lilith,' said Conall simply.

'But, Lilith is the statue in–'

'Lilith,' he repeated, as the large barn owl swooped down towards them.

Chapter 9

Ailsa watched in surprise and with a little trepidation as the ghostly-pale owl swooped over their heads and landed on another beam behind them. They turned to look at her.

'Lilith' breathed Ailsa quietly as she took in the magnificent bird's appearance. Mostly white, very large and imperious-looking, she stared down at them with a mild curiosity.

'Have we interrupted her sleep?' she whispered to Conall without moving.

'Possibly,' he whispered back, moving disturbingly close to her ear, 'but barn owls will occasionally hunt in the daytime too. It will be dusk soon, so she might start her hunting then.'

'She's called after the statue, then?'

' Mm,' was the non-committal answer.

She turned to look at him.

'Or the other way around,' he continued.

Ailsa didn't see how this was possible given the age of the statue. Another thought occurred to her.

'The thatchers! Will they disturb her home?'

'They might but don't worry, there are the other ruined outbuildings on this land or maybe a hollow tree.'

As if to prove the point, they watched Lilith glide down silently, out through the gaping hole in the roof and over to the stand of trees on the hill, where she remained.

'That is one of her favourite roosts,' he smiled. How did he know so much about her? Remembering, she thought aloud.

'Chanter's Hill?'

Conall frowned.

'Yes, Chanter's Hill,' he said, his voice low. She looked at the old stone wall beyond the barn, almost ruined now, but it was a definite separation of her land and the land beyond.

'It's not mine, though,' she remembered.

'Oh yes, it is,' he growled, surprising Ailsa.

'But on the deeds...'

'Chanter's Hill belongs to this land. It belongs to Nightowl's Hide… to Effie.'

'But legally?'

'There is nothing legal about it where the Haighs are concerned,' He breathed down his nose and Ailsa was reminded of a thoroughbred horse snorting in annoyance. 'Have you heard of Boaz Haigh?'

Apart from a terse 'talk to Sylvia', she could get no more out of him except, 'or Margaret Harker.'

She looked up sharply at him.

'Margaret Harker? That's Peggy Harker, isn't it, from Farstone?'

He nodded.

How do you–?

He clamped his lips together and turned to walk back down to the village. She didn't want to upset him with more questions when he had only just started talking to her. She ran up to join him.

'As a matter of fact, I'm there tomorrow at Gallipot Cottage, to see the Wildflower meadow on the first day of spring.'

He seemed to relax a little.

'The Wildflower Witch?'

'You know Flora?'

'I've heard of her, but there's been a Wildflower Witch at Gallipot for centuries. I know of her partner more.'

'Cal – Calum?'

'Yes, he's a cousin of sorts.'

' I didn't realise you were related to him.'

Ailsa could see a similarity in looks, even if it was only that they were both devastatingly good-looking.

'We're all related,' he said mysteriously.

*

Ailsa thought about this last statement of Conall's as she drove towards Farstone the next morning, sans hangover. She hoped it didn't mean that she was related to him. She wanted to keep her options open in that direction. Also, who was this Boaz Haigh that she had to ask Peggy about?

She banished these thoughts from her head in favour of concentration as she negotiated the tricky, steep, winding, single-track road that was the only way in or out of Farstone village. Farstone Moors surrounded it. The same moor which bordered Hatton-le-Hollow.

She parked in the Peverel Arms car park and called in for her aunt Philippa and cousin Mary. Jerry was looking after the bar, but most people were going to be crowded in Flora's little cottage on the patio outside. Luckily, it was a warm spring-like day, apt and hopefully an omen of things to come very soon.

As Ailsa rounded the back of Gallipot Cottage, she was rewarded by a view of the huge herb and flower garden that had been there when she was a

78

child and apparently for hundreds of years before. It took her breath away. Even at this time of year. It was colourful and incredibly beautiful. She remembered being taken there when she was a child by Philippa, but Flora had made it much better. She used it for her natural healing business, so she had to keep on top of it.

She was ambushed by Jennet Cayley, Flora's aunt and the sister of her late mother Matilda. She asked her all about Nightowl's Hide while her twins. Emma and John toddled round at their feet. Next came Binky Peverel, who introduced Ailsa to her brother, Sir Ralph Peverel, whom she couldn't recall. He had apparently travelled extensively until he found out that Flora was his daughter, but then he came home to be near her.

She asked Binky if she'd seen Peggy, but she had popped back to her own cottage just down the lane from Gallipot. Ailsa escaped and grabbed a cup of coffee. She was just thinking that Conall was right and everyone, at least in these villages on the edge of Farstone Moor, was related. It was a sobering thought, and so was the fact that she knew that many of the people here were witches. Now that really *was* a thought to keep to yourself outside these parts of Yorkshire. Even in these supposedly enlightened times, people might not understand.

She wasn't actually sure that *she* understood. In the spirit of letting go of the past and shaking off the influence of her mother, she really ought to make an effort to comprehend it all. She really must talk to Peggy.

'There you are!' Flora came up to her smiling.

Ailsa spread her arm to indicate the Wildflower meadow.

'This is wonderful. I can't ever remember it looking this good.'

'Thank you, I'm rather proud of it, but of course, the hard work had been done before I arrived here. But that wasn't what I wanted to talk to you about. How did you know I was pregnant? I had only told close family and I know Philippa wouldn't have told you.'

Ailsa was thrown for a moment and fell back on her excuse to herself at the time.

'It's because you weren't drinking alcohol.'

'How do you know I didn't drink alcohol anyway?'

Flora's eyes narrowed, but there was a teasing smile on her face.

'I don't know then, just something about the way you held yourself. Anyway, how's it going?'

'It's fine,' said Flora, recognising defeat. 'I'm not that far on, but everything is going well.'

'Of course it is. She'll be a lovely, healthy baby.' Ailsa smiled. It took them both a moment or two to let this sink in.

'She?' said Flora in a wavery voice.

'Or – or he,' stammered Ailsa.

Flora looked confused, then happy, then incredibly happy.

'You don't know how much that means to me. I don't seem to be able to 'see' anything myself, which was worrying me,' and she gave her a big hug.

What on earth had made Ailsa tell her that? What if she was mistaken or even if something went wrong, like with Flora's own mother. How would she feel then? She *must* stop doing this – but it just seemed to come out of her mouth of its own accord.

'I haven't had a hug yet,' came the gentle voice of Flora's father.

'Oh Dad, this is …'

'We've met,' he laughed, 'I hope you're enjoying yourself, Ailsa? I was just looking for Cal.'

'He's around somewhere,' said Flora, 'ah, there.'

Clad in jeans and a white shirt and looking, frankly, very handsome, he was walking down the meadow from the direction of Pookey Wood at the top. He had an arm full of herbs, which he handed over to Flora.

'The first comfrey of the year, my lady,' he grinned and Ailsa's heart melted as she saw the look of pure love exchanged between them. She watched as Cal and Ralph fell into an amicable conversation as they walked off.

An arm linked through hers as her cousin Mary pulled her towards the meadow.

'Come and have a look,' she said enthusiastically. 'There's not a lot of colour yet, but you wait a month or so. I'm allowed to sow a lot of the seeds now, so I can show you what will be growing.' Mary led her off proudly as Ailsa and Flora exchanged grins. Mary had an innocence about her which suddenly reminded her of Star.

She pointed out various plants, some still in the early stages of growing, but they all looked the same to Ailsa. She supposed this was another thing she ought to get used to, as there were quite a lot of herbs growing wild at Nightowl's Hide. This prompted a memory of the night spent at Star's cottage, one she had forgotten.

Star had drunkenly admitted to frequently harvesting herbs from the garden, but only before Ailsa had bought it. They were just going begging, so Ailsa was fairly sure she had invited her to take them whenever she wanted. She doubted Star would remember, though. She chuckled to herself.

She saw that Mary had stopped to talk to a plump blonde lady, who looked very much like Arnie Peterson, Mary's fiancé, so was probably his mother. She looked like she might be quite a while - probably talking wedding plans- so Ailsa carried on towards Pookey Wood.

She remembered that Flora's mother's ashes were spread there. She also remembered Matty herself, who had died around the time that Ailsa left Farstone and she recalled a placid, smiling person who didn't deserve to go so young, so she would like to pay her respects.

Chapter 10

Leaves were already showing on the trees in the wood. She didn't know where the ashes were scattered - or buried - so she just said a silent blessing in her mind, telling Matty that she was having a grandchild. The fact that she knew in her mind that the baby would be healthy and a girl alarmed her considerably, but now, it seemed to give her hope that everything would be alright for Flora. She tried to clear her mind of any thoughts of seeing the future though, because, given the reputation of Farstone, "that way madness lies".

She turned towards the meadow again, noticing through the trees that Mary and the blonde lady were still in intense conversation. Out of the corner of her eye, she saw something. Not saw, that was the wrong word, became aware of something. When she turned her head, she jumped as she saw the same hooded man who had been talking to

Conall the other day. Something deep in her mind clicked. She dredged her memories. He had been around the village a few times when she was a child. Possibly a vagrant. He seemed old because of the long, ragged clothes he wore, almost from another era, but when he moved, it was with the energy and litheness of a younger man. Nobody could recall seeing his face to determine his age, which was a Very Strange Thing. The Storyteller, he was called, and to the children of Farstone, he was like a bogeyman. But she was grown up now and didn't believe in bogeymen, did she? She would put the fear to rest and go over and talk to him.

He watched her approach. At least, he was facing towards her, thought. Ailsa, though she couldn't make out any features. They were probably in shadow as his hood was pulled right over, covering where his face was.

'Ailsa Reed,' a stern voice called her from the meadow. 'I want to talk to you.'

She glanced to her left and saw Peggy standing on the grass path in front of the wood. When she looked back, the hooded man had gone. Disappeared. How could he hide in these sparse trees or move so quickly that he'd be out of sight now? She turned round 360 degrees before Peggy's voice called out again.

'Where did he go?' she asked when she joined. Peggy.

'Who?' replied Peggy. Innocence didn't sit well on her shoulders.

'The Storyteller,' Ailsa tried.

'Oh, Culhain? He comes, he goes. Best not to trouble yourself.'

'What did you want, Peggy?' Ailsa felt annoyed. She knew Peggy was keeping things from her. She was usually a little scared of Peggy - and probably would be again in 5 minutes- but at the moment, annoyance overcame fear.

'Bianca said you were looking for me,' she said without smiling.

Bianca was Binky's real name, like Ailsa was always Ailsa Reed and not McKendry. Peggy always liked to call everyone by their real name, which was weird as everyone called her Peggy, not Margaret. If she talked to herself behind closed doors though, thought Ailsa, she would lay odds that she called herself Margaret.

'Oh yes I did. Conall told me to talk to you.'

At Conall's name, Peggy's eyes flew up to the wood and swiftly back again.

'Or Sylvia, who is the vicar's wife in Hatton-le-Hollow, who everyone seems to be telling me to talk to.'

'What about?

A woman of few words our Peggy.

'Everyone being related, I think? Oh yes, Boaz Haigh?'

'Conall told you?' Peggy said shortly.

'Yes,' said Ailsa. Two could play at this game.

'Follow me,' and the older woman led the way back down to Gallipot Cottage. Peggy sat on a bench next to a hedge at the far side of the garden, away from most of the guests, as Ailsa joined her. She opened her mouth to speak but Ailsa got it in first.

'*Are* we all related? Conall said we were.'

'Did he? Farstone is a small village which used to be cut off during the winter months, all the way up to Victorian times.'

'And even now' Ailsa smiled wryly, thinking of being snowed in at Philippa's one Christmas.

'That is so,' acknowledged Peggy, 'it is an inaccessible place and long ago, families married into another local family instead of going further afield, before Farstone was even big enough to be called a village. Not inbred, but intermingled. The marriages were often performed by the Squire as we have no church here. Over the years, blood inevitably became mixed at some point, to an inconsequential degree.

'The same families still live here. The same names live on in the Gardwickes, the Harkers, the

87

Peverels, the Reeds, the Petersons... Look at the colour of your hair. A dirty blonde, like your father's…'

'Some people are kinder than you and call it straw coloured, or even in summer, "like the sun shining on the wheat field" too,' Ailsa was stung to reply.

'So, this dirty blonde,' continued Peggy, 'is probably a mix of the blonde of the Peterson family who came over with the Vikings and the black hair of the early Celtic settlers, the Gardwickes. With the light brown, Anglo-Saxon hair of the Peverels thrown in for good measure.'

'Oh my God, Mary is going to marry Arnie Peterson. Is it incest?' Ailsa was appalled.

'Calm down, madam. If there was any inbreeding, it is from centuries ago and has diluted so much that if they are cousins - and they probably are - they are cousins many times removed. You would have the same odds of marrying a cousin many times removed if you went to a city and married a stranger. Most of us in this country and others are related in some age-old way. But, as you're asking, probably a little more in Farstone.'

'Conall was saying he was Cal's cousin, of sorts. Could he be related to me?' Ailsa blurted out. For some reason that she didn't want to think about, the answer was important to her.

'No, Cal and Conall are... different, but just possibly related to each other, although I'm not sure Cal knows that - and Conall shouldn't have been randomly throwing this information about, so don't mention it to Cal.'

Ailsa frowned. All rather strange, she thought, but promised all the same.

'And the Storyteller?'

Peggy stiffened.

'Culhain is different again. Not related to them - but with the same ancestry.'

Ailsa was just going to ask how that worked as surely if they had the same ancestry then…, when Peggy got up, dismissing the subject, as far as she was concerned.

'As for Boaz Haigh, you're better off talking to my cousin about that. She's sitting there sunning herself in the chair under the small window.'

Ailsa saw a tall, elegant woman, dressed immaculately, with her silver hair swept back in a chignon and her eyes closed, soaking up what could be the last of the sun for a while at this time of year. Ailsa grinned.

'Another cousin, Peggy?'

'We share a great-grandfather. Like I say, cousin twice removed, although she *is* a Harker,' she said importantly and with that, she was off.

Going to spread a little of her infectious happiness elsewhere, Ailsa chuckled to herself, although she supposed she was quite fond of the old bat in a way. Then she worried that Peggy had been able to read her mind, even with her back to her.

*

Ailsa went into the kitchen to make a cup of tea and found Chilvers, the Peverel's old nanny, handing them out. She grabbed one before Chilvers spilt it all in the saucer- she must have been in her nineties now, surely - and went outside to grab the seat next to Peggy's cousin.

'Hello,' she said, standing in front of her. The woman's eyes sprang open, She really had been asleep, thought Ailsa. 'I'm sorry I've startled you. I didn't realise.'

'It's quite all right, dear. Oh, good heavens, I must have reached that age where I drop to sleep at random times during the day. Soon, my nose will be constantly dribbling and I'll have to carry a hankie with me permanently, shoved up my sleeve and half falling out.'

Ailsa stared, then burst out laughing. You could tell she was twice removed from Peggy. In fact, she seemed twenty times removed, in appearance and manner.

'Ailsa McKendry.' She put her hand out.

'Ah,' she said as though she recognised her, although she didn't look the Folk festival type. They shook hands.

'Born Ailsa Reed, Philippa's niece,' she added.

'Ah,' the woman said in a 'now I know who you are' voice and indicated the seat next to her.

'Peggy said I should talk to you about Boaz Haigh?'

The woman's face, attractive for her age, clouded over. She must have been younger than Peggy. Either that or she had worn much better.

'That man and his descendants have been nothing but trouble. He's the one who persecuted Effie Scritchell.' She suddenly smiled and her eyes twinkled. 'Sorry about that. The Haigh family are my bête noir.'

She leaned across to Ailsa, suddenly serious again.

'Can I ask, do you believe a family can be inherently evil, with the evil built into their genes throughout time?'

A serious question deserved a serious answer, so Ailsa thought for a minute.

'I think that some families do appear to be evil throughout the generations,' she paused, 'but how much of that is caused by outside influences?'

91

'Oh God, you're not an amateur psychologist, are you?' said the woman, sitting back.

'Far from it. I would never have thought of myself that way, but you asked me a question and one thought led to another.'

The older woman screwed her eyes up and looked amused. 'Go on,' she said.

'Well, this family, let's call them Haigh....'

She looked up as the woman grinned at her. She was as outspoken as Peggy was, but she could definitely get to like her. She had a sense of humour for a start.

'This family have been evil for many generations, unrelentingly so, for as far back as anyone can remember. There is no doubt about that. Yet are they evil because they felt they had to live up to their reputation, or because of pressure from their family to conform to their stereotype?'

Peggy's cousin folded her arms, only half agreeing. She was a hard audience.

'Or, was it because something happened *before* anyone can remember. Something so traumatic that it became embedded in their collective memories?'

'I'm listening,' said the woman, and she was, intently.

'What if, say in Neolithic times, a small Haigh son witnessed the whole of his family being slaughtered by someone? If it didn't send him mad, the deed could have imprinted itself on his psyche and resounded over thousands of years in the cold, vengeful hearts of that family. So, in that case, would you say that the family is evil, or that perhaps evil was thrust upon them?'

'The Carl Jung Foundation for Analytical Psychology missed a trick not getting you in there,' the woman laughed, ' but yes, nothing is ever black and white, is it?'

'Boaz Haigh, did anything happen to turn him evil and make him act against Effie like he did?'

'Ohhh.'

The sound was drawn out and she sat back against the wall and closed her eyes. Was she going to sleep again? Without opening her eyes, she said,

'Yes, his young daughter died.'

'Oh, poor man.'

'Agreed,' she said, sitting upright with her eyes flying open,' but Effie had nothing to do with it and, what's more, I think he must have known it deep down.'

'He just wanted to take it out on someone,' Ailsa nodded.

'Yes, but life isn't like that. You can't go and get someone killed because they were near your relative when they died. God-fearing people should accept that it was God's will and not blame anyone. Instead, perhaps they could blame circumstances and disease instead. We can try to understand the man while still condemning the act.'

'I agree with you.' Ailsa said.

'Have you met Dinsmore Haigh yet?'

'No,' Ailsa frowned, 'Is he from Hatton too?'

'Yes, and alive and kicking. You might change your mind about inherent evil when you *do* meet him,' she grimaced.

Ailsa laughed.

'Another thing I've got to ask Sylvia about then.'

'Sylvia?'

'Yes, the vicar's wife in my village. Everyone, including Conall and Star, my next-door neighbour, has told me to ask Sylvia about Effie and Boaz Haigh. She sounds knowledgeable but also a tad imperious, as though she owns the village. Although it's been mostly emails and a brief phone call, so I shouldn't judge on that, should I?'

'You should apply some of your own psychology to the situation,' the woman smiled. She was looking at Ailsa as though she was weighing her up. She suddenly seemed to come to a decision.

'Come and see me next week if you can. I can tell you all about Effie and the other witches, too.'

'Just Effie will do, I think. And that would really be lovely, thank you. I'd much rather talk to you than this Sylvia. I feel like we get on well.'

'We do,' she nodded and smiled warmly at Ailsa.

'Anytime next week?'

'Possibly the latter half?'

'Where do you live?'

Peggy's cousin pulled out a small notebook from her handbag and wrote something on a page before tearing it out.

'Thanks,' she said as the woman turned to walk over to Peggy.

Ailsa looked up the paper. The note said in beautiful copperplate handwriting. ***Sylvia Pennyquick, The Vicarage, Hatton-le-Hollow.***

Too late, Ailsa recognised the cut-glass accent from the phone call months ago. Her face fell and she looked up as Sylvia threw her a quick wink, her shoulders shaking with silent laughter.

Chapter 11

With her head down and her hands deep in her pockets, Ailsa marched across the moor at a pace more suited to a road race and not for a walk amongst scrubby brown heather that waited to trip you up and sprain your ankle.

She thought about what had happened this morning on her trip to Pickering. She drove in to buy food and collect an order of an ethnic throw from an independent home furnishings shop. Her home had looked strangely clinical after spending time in Star's cosy cottage. She wasn't about to start painting everything pink and mauve, but she was going to make an effort to add colour.

This was Ailsa McKendry, who hadn't cared about what her flat looked like before as long as it was practical. This place was having a strange effect on her.

As she had wandered past the Town Hall, laden with bags, a woman handing leaflets out had come across and rudely shoved one in her bag, right at the top of the chicken chow mein ready meal.

'Are you from around here?' she asked, almost accusingly.

Ailsa took in the woman's appearance. A smart white woollen coat rested over her expansive bust. Her gold bracelets jangled together on her thick wrists. Her hair, dyed red, was immaculately coiffured in the style of Mrs. Slocombe in Are You Being Served. Her mouth was pursed like she was sucking an acid drop- and Ailsa disliked her on sight.

'Yes,' she answered shortly.

'Well, you'll be interested in this then. You'll know of Hatton-le-Hollow?'

Ailsa's face remained immobile, if slightly annoyed.

'I've heard of it,' she replied.

'Now this 'incomer' has moved into the village and she plans to stage a huge music festival there. The village will be invaded by all sorts of unsavoury people from far and wide. The peace of the village will be shattered, as will all the residents who have had loud, raucous music ringing in their ears for three days. THREE DAYS!'

She went towards Ailsa and shouted this at twenty decibels, her tiny piggy eyes shining and her sense of entitlement in full flow. She continued.

'I implore you to help these poor residents to avoid this atrocity.'

She couldn't speak. Eventually, she managed a smile, which to an onlooker was like that of the crocodile before it ate Captain Hook's hand - and she walked off as slowly as she could manage, in the opposite direction. This was incredibly hard as the only thing she felt impelled to do was run back to the woman and shove her leaflets where the sun don't shine.

This was why now, after depositing the bags at home, she was walking across Farstone Moor as though the devil himself were after her.

She didn't know how far she'd walked but she found herself in a dip, a shallow vale, with the edge of a band of trees to her right. The woods were quite extensive, which, to a lot of people, would seem a strange thing to occur on a moor. Yet, she had long known that the North York Moors had suffered from deforestation many years ago, starting in the Neolithic age and leaving mostly moorland by the 12th to 13th centuries. Trees had only survived in these fertile depressions in the land. Amongst others, there were hazel, birch and rowan trees.

As she approached them, she could make out a cross between a shepherd's hut and a gypsy caravan, near the edge of the treeline. Fascinated, she slowed her furious pace and walked quietly towards it. There was no sign of life, so, lacking the courage to knock at the door, she started to walk past it. Then she heard a noise to her right, where the trees curved around.

There stood the somewhat regal figure of Conall, tall, erect and assured. He was holding his arm out. She gasped and stood stock still. From the trees, which were only now bursting into life, came a creature which she half-recognised as a deer, a stag. What stopped her from recognising it as normal was that it was pure white. Even to the antlers.

It was delicate, exquisite, and it took graceful steps towards the man's hand, where it accepted that hand on the side of its head, allowing Conall's head to rest against its own. Ailsa hardly dared breathe. Never had she felt as much like an intruder as she did now. It felt like a very private moment.

Conall and the white stag separated and faced each other. It seemed to Ailsa, frozen where she stood, that they were having a silent communication between them, especially when

Conall nodded and the stag raised its head, then its right hoof, striking the ground three times before it melted back amongst the trees.

Conall stood there a little while longer, staring into the woods and then began to turn around. He seemed to Ailsa's guilty mind to look over her in her direction, although he didn't seem to notice anything. In a panic, she dropped to the ground, hiding behind some scrubby heather tufts in a hollow. She lifted her eyes to see Conall stroll towards the hut and round to the front, which was facing her. He climbed up the two steps, opened the door and went in.

She made a quick dash to the tree line further behind her and, keeping out of sight of the windows on the side of the hut. Risking a sprained ankle, she ran as fast as she could towards Hatton, only slowing down after five minutes, when she could begin to breathe normally at last.

She had at least solved the question of where Conall lived, but other questions had presented themselves now that were more important than Conall's current abode.

*

Although she felt she had walked her anger off, in reality, it probably disappeared when she saw the white stag and Conall. How could anyone stay angry after they had witnessed such beauty,

100

such gentleness? It was one of those things that would always stay with you throughout your life.

She felt oddly off balance. The vitriol of the woman this morning against the peace of man and beast had made her unsettled. Should she visit Sylvia? No, she wouldn't take in all the information she wanted from her at the moment. Should she just go home and read or watch TV? She wouldn't be able to concentrate. What she needed was some pleasant company from someone who demanded neither attention nor concentration.

And so it was that she found herself knocking on Star's door. She was surprised to find that she was disappointed when no one answered. She went around the back and peered through the kitchen window.

'Star?' she shouted and was just about to give up when she heard a growl behind her. She turned quickly to see Charm(less) peering up at her through slitted, judgemental eyes. What? How can a cat growl? She wouldn't put anything past this particular cat, though.

Raising its imperious nose, it gave her one last look of disgust before it waddled off down the garden, swaying its quivering bulk as it went. She followed it, reasoning that Star might be down there. As they reached the end of the garden, possibly a hundred yards long, she saw the cat go to the hedge which bordered Ailsa's own land and then completely disappear. How had it pulled its bulk through the hedge?

As she came opposite, she could see there was a gap in the hedge. Natural or man-made, she wasn't sure. She might as well use it to go home now, so she stepped through to find herself roughly where the wall separating her own piece of garden from the rest of her land would be built. In fact, the landscapers had already pegged out the boundary.

Ailsa looked to her right to see where Charm(less) had gone and saw it walking past the car park site would be, where it disappeared behind a clump of trees. She followed. When she got there. There was no sign of the enormous cat - and it was hard to miss.

She carried on towards the large brick outhouse that would be transformed very soon into a washhouse and started to walk forward. She heard a voice behind it and she trod softly so as not to alarm Star.

'I wondered where you'd gone, Charm, you big softie.'

Softie? thought Ailsa.

'Have you come to help me then? Have you?' It was at this moment that Star noticed Ailsa, who was unaware of the effect it would have.

Star threw her basket up in the air in shock, greenery from it falling all over her, while giving a loud squeal like a stuck pig.

Charm(less) jumped in the air, all four limbs stretched out as though it had been given an electric shock. Ailsa felt like she was watching an episode of Tom and Jerry.

'What...?' she asked.

'I'm sorry...' Star said at the same time, picking her basket from the ground while Ailsa picked leafy greens from the girl's hair.

'Sorry for what? I didn't mean to make you jump.' Although noticing Charm(less) shooting metaphorical daggers at her through its eyes, she held back a snigger.

'I'm sorry for being in your garden and taking your herbs. I've been using them ever since I moved in, for cooking- and for Green Witch spells – and for dandelion juice…' She immediately regretted mentioning the juice, 'I didn't mean to trespass.'

She was almost in tears.

Ailsa put her hands in the air in a 'stop' gesture.

'It's okay. It's okay. It doesn't matter at all. I thought I'd said you could use the herbs that night at your cottage, but you obviously haven't remembered.'

They looked at each other, neither sure of what had actually been said.

'I'm glad you're getting some use out of it anyway before it's tidied up…'

'Tidied up?'

'Yes, just after this outhouse, is where the festival will be held, with the camping site just here. I'm cutting it all back so it's neat and tidy for them to camp and walk on.'

Star looked horrified.

'Neat? And tidy?' She repeated slowly.

Ailsa frowned and kept silent.

'No. You can't destroy these herb beds. They've probably been there since Effie Scritchell's time. She probably gathered her herbs from the very same places as I have. And there are some lovely wildflowers growing in all this long grass too. Please, Ailsa, please?'

Those big eyes pleaded with her.

'And,' she continued. 'Will the festival goers, who'll come to listen to mostly traditional folk songs whose origins are steeped in history and legend, want *neat and tidy*?'

Star looked aghast.

Ailsa thought then of the people who liked and played the old songs and decided that Star was right. Neat and tidy wouldn't matter to them.

Then, she thought of her own new cottage, which was very neat, tidy and shiny and decided that that wasn't her either. She wanted a home, not a showpiece- and she hoped Effie would forgive her for sanitising the place.

Then she thought of Flora's wildflower meadow and the pleasure she received when she saw it and she decided that, in some small way, she would pay homage to it.

'You're right, Star. The herbs stay and people will walk around them. I can't leave all the grass this long, but I can leave it to grow longer with natural native wildflowers growing near to the hedges – and swathes of wildflower grass growing, with shorter grass paths weaving round them, perhaps. And large spaces with shorter grass in the middle and at the top, where the stage and the audience will be. I will leave as much as I possibly can. Will that be all right?'

Star had been standing open-mouthed.

'I can't tell you how all right that is. It's fantastic!' and then she burst into tears.

Oh God. Well, Ailsa had a good way to distract her.

'And would you mind doing me a favour? Will you come and have a cup of tea in Nightowl's Hide and give me some tips on making my home more warm and welcoming, like yours is?'

105

Star obviously thought Ailsa had taken leave of her senses but when she checked that she wasn't joking, she managed to nod her head, while Ailsa grabbed hold of her arm to guide her towards the cottage, followed by an enormous and still-disgruntled marmalade cat whose dignity had taken a dive, and privately thought that Ailsa had crept up on them on purpose.

Chapter 12

An hour later, Ailsa had written down a few of Star's ideas to put colour and cosiness in Nightowl's Hide- and rejected just as many, although she pretended to write them down seriously. She had learnt that Star was a sensitive soul as well as being a very warm human being. She had also learnt that Charm(less) wouldn't enter her cottage, which Ailsa thought was a Very Good Thing.

They had drunk chamomile and honey tea, albeit from tea bags out of a box. Just as Star was leaving, she addressed Ailsa.

'Will you come into Star Cottage with me? I want to try something.'

Ailsa frowned, looking unsure.

'If it's food. I'm not feeling...'

'No, it's not food.'

Thank goodness for that, thought. Ailsa..

I thought of something that might help you relax.'

'Not more alcohol?'

'No! Follow me.'

So she did follow the multicoloured figure, decked out in the long, rainbow dress, accompanied by a clunking noise as her bracelets, pendants and earrings made their own discordant music. Charm(less) sat at the kitchen door, giving Star a reproachful look as she let her in.

Star pointed to one of the chairs. Ailsa could see the cat making for the chair and sprinted so she got there first. There was a growl.

'There it is again. Your cat growls.'

'It just sounds like a growl. It's actually a sound she makes when she's happy.

Ailsa looked down at the cat's face. A piercing stare, neck thrust forward, lips drawn back to reveal sharp teeth. Happy wasn't what even the most ardent cat lover would call that face.

'First,' and Star put two drinks down on the table. They were in wooden cups with symbols hand-carved into them. Ailsa had noticed wooden spoons and wooden placemats with the same symbols on them.

'It's not–?'

'–alcohol? No! I told you that won't happen again. It's purely herbs and honey, an old recipe that Peggy gave me, handed down in her family.'

'Peggy? My Peggy?'

' Oh, are you related?'

Ailsa looked confused for a moment.

'No, I meant the one from Farstone.'

Star nodded and Ailsa wondered what on earth had possessed her to call Peggy 'hers'. Maybe she was coming to terms with the old trout now that time had passed.

Star produced a local paper that she had mentioned to Ailsa. In it was a, thankfully, brief piece about her festivals and the meeting to try and ban them. Above it was a picture of two people, one of whom was the harpy who had accosted her earlier. She looked into the camera with a dazzling smile. Her head tilted at an angle as though she were on a modelling assignment. The man next to her had a face that would scare small children and fluffy household pets, with the exception of Charm(less), who would probably scare him.

The caption read 'Mr Dinsmore Haigh, head of the Stop The Festival committee and his wife, Ludmilla (Lulu).'

'Lulu?' grunted Ailsa, 'is that ironic?'

'Ludmilla thinks it's an affectionate nickname from school, but Sylvia, who went to school with

109

her, said that they called her that because she always used to shout and was incapable of speaking quietly.'

As she said this, Star looked at Ailsa for enlightenment, which Ailsa couldn't provide.

'I didn't understand either, but Sylvia said I would have had to have been around in the 1960s to get it.'

A while later, even though they had been talking about the upcoming meeting and the possibility of having no festivals, she felt strangely relaxed.

'Are you sure...?'

'How many more times? No alcohol! It's the herbs themselves that are relaxing you. Do you want another?'

She realised that she did and holding both full wooden goblets, she followed Star through the kitchen door and out behind her cottage into the garden. She noticed that Star also carried a shoulder bag and a small metal bowl of water. They went to the gap in the hedge and stepped through.

'Where are we going?'

'You need to be on your own property for this to work.' Star said mysteriously. 'Where on your land do you feel is a special place for you?'

Ailsa looked blank, Star tried again.

'Somewhere that makes you feel different when you're there. That makes your heart give a little jump. Even a place that you think is attractive and pleases you.'

Ailsa's mind went back to the first time she had come across the old round barn. The moment she had entered it, even though there wasn't much left intact, she had felt a great feeling of peace, of connection. She shut her eyes, remembering.

Connection? Then she realised that the barn was where she felt the closest connection to Effie Scritchell. Now Lilith was in residence, it felt even more special. Her eyes opened.

'Yes, the round barn.'

Star smiled.

'Then that's where we'll go.'

*

On the walk up to the top of the land, Star asked her to pick up any small, natural things that appealed to her and carry them up with her.

And so it was that Ailsa ended up with a selection of smooth stones, a laurel leaf for luck, a small piece of wood from underneath the silver birch and a twig in the shape of a 'Y' in her pockets.

There was also what looked suspiciously like a stone arrowhead next to the same tree and mostly buried, its edges chipped away to form a point with the two corners of the triangle barbed. They were both very excited about this particular find.

Just before they reached the barn, Ailsa saw something glinting in the light from under a hedge and picked up a piece of silver metal that almost looked like the shape of a leaf. She thought she might take that up to the cottage and put it on one of her silver chains, as it looked so delicate that it might get lost from the altar.

They entered the building, which was almost done now. In fact, the thatchers were finishing off in the next day or two.

'Where did you get that feeling most?'

Ailsa looked around.

'Everywhere really. Probably in the middle, but anywhere in the barn, it doesn't matter.'

'Well, the fire would have been in the centre so, further towards the edges? Is that okay?'

Ailsa looked in surprise at this new, confident and possibly intelligent Star.

'Yes, yes that's fine,' although she still didn't know what they were doing there.

'Now this piece of wood here.' Star picked up a broad piece of what could have been a scaffolding board that the thatchers had left. 'This can be your altar.'

'Not witchy stuff, please,' pleaded Ailsa, 'you know how I feel about that.'

'I know how your mother felt about it. I don't think you feel the same.'

So in deference to this scarily insightful Star, she shut up and built her own altar according to Star's instructions. At the end, Star produced matches and three candles, one gold, one green and one black.

'My gifts to you,' She said, holding them towards Ailsa. 'They have to be yours.'

Ailsa placed them on the altar at intervals, amongst the other objects, lighting the matches and melting the ends of the candles so they remained in place. Then she lit the wicks.

'You can gradually make the altar your own, adding pieces if you feel a connection.'

Ailsa gave her a withering look.

'Anyway,' she said,' what is this all for?'

'We're going to see if you can get rid of your negativity, find a psychic connection between the earth and the spirits to help you - and see if you can envision your festivals, so you will know that it will happen?'

'Is that all? Said Ailsa sarcastically, 'No problem then.

It went over Star's head, as usual.

Chapter 13

'Ailsa!' said Star as firmly as she could, as it didn't come easily to her. 'Stop giggling and repeat each line after me. It won't work if you don't take it seriously.'

A spell, thought. Ailsa? Really? She was starting to regret moving back to this part of Yorkshire if all this sort of stuff started rearing its head again. The chanting of the spell had set her off laughing.

She looked at Star's face. Oh God, her eyes were shiny with tears again. She was *so* sensitive. She was only trying to help her in her own way and Ailsa felt bad for laughing. She composed her features, took a deep breath and prepared herself.

'Shall we try again?' Star sounded like a prim schoolmistress. 'You may not be able to look ahead and see your festival outcome if you don't give it a good try. You could even ask a question, you know? Or ask for a good outcome for the festival.'

Then she did the nearest thing to a harrumph that a small, kind, green witch could do.

'I'm ready.' Ailsa replied, trying not to look at her.

'Pick something from the altar, hold it in your hand and repeat after me. –

*

'Grant me knowledge.'

Ailsa repeated it throughout.

'To find hope for the future,

To vanquish opposition,

To keep darkness out,

To show me the light,

To resolve obstacles that stand in my way.

Encircle my life, my home

And grant me knowledge.'

*

Ailsa sat with her eyes shut for a moment or two after, waiting for Star to speak. There was no sound, and the silence seemed to stretch on forever. She felt blackness as though she were falling asleep. Suddenly, the piece of wood in her hand became warm and her eyes opened slowly. She looks straight into the flames of all three candles, which seem to blend together as one. There was nothing else, only blackness and the flames.

Words formed in her mind. *I need guidance.* She felt her lips move, but heard no sound. Gradually, within the flames, she could make out two figures. Two men. One, shadowy, with thick bushy hair, was half hidden. He held his hand out and the other man shook it with a strange handshake.

The other bespectacled man had on a shiny blue suit and his hair was wispy. There was a large sack on the desk between them with large, shiny gold coins spilling out of it like pirates' gold.

Then she was gasping, being drawn backwards through a tunnel, the flame receding until, once again, she sat opposite the three flames, standing some distance apart on the altar. She could feel someone shaking her.

'Ailsa, Ailsa, are you all right? Answer me.' Star shouted in a panic.

Ailsa turned to her slowly as though she'd been woken from a long sleep and her eyes eventually focused on the stricken face in front of her.

'Oh, thank God for that! I thought- I don't know what I thought. That you were in a trance.' Star abruptly stopped talking. 'Oh, I see. You were having me on, weren't you? Trying to teach me a lesson?'

Star looked like she really hoped the answer would be yes, but Ailsa couldn't oblige.

'No. I wasn't having you on.'

She still felt as though she wasn't there.

'Really? Did you feel something?'

'I saw something.'

'You saw something? Will the festival go ahead? You *saw* something? You really are a witch, aren't you?'

'Oh for heaven's sake.' Ailsa came to and pushed herself up, wobbling slightly, 'Don't say that.'

'You're not mad with me, are you?'

'No, I'm not mad with you. Just feeling incredibly wiped out at the moment. Come on, I need a drink - definitely without dandelion in it.'

Star followed her like a naughty little girl who'd been given detention. Ailsa said over her shoulder.

'And can you make sure those candles are completely extinguished? I don't want the barn burning down when I'm only just restoring it.'

Star scuttled off to do as she was told.

*

The next morning, Ailsa felt normal again. Star hadn't stopped apologising all evening but veered between that and excitement that Ailsa was following in her ancestor's footsteps, (Ailsa put a stop this train of thought straight away), and a little bit of peevishness that 'nothing like that has ever happened to me', even though she'd been trying for two years.

Ailsa was now going to do what the whole of North Yorkshire, or so it seemed, had suggested and talk to Sylvia. Not being able to face yet another apology from Star, she let herself out of the rarely used front door.

There was a parcel on the doormat of the covered wooden porch, which had sheltered the bright yellow paper package from the early morning drizzle. She stepped back into the house and opened it. It was a lovely, hand-knitted, green and yellow cushion cover from Star. She smiled and looked at the accompanying card. 'Sorry!!!', it said. Ailsa sighed and continued on her way to the vicarage.

She had seen the building from the roadside before, but because it was up a gravel drive and mostly shielded from sight by a laurel hedge, this was the first time she had taken it in properly.

A detached, stone-built house faced her at the end of the driveway. It stood foursquare and was like a larger version of a child's drawing. Three windows across the top and a door downstairs with a large mullioned window on each side. Chimneys rose at the front and back of the slate roof and there was a large arched chapel-style window on the gable end nearest to her. One strange addition was that of a bell tower, almost mirroring the one at the church. It looked a friendly place somehow.

She lifted the brass door knocker and gave three loud raps.

'Stop that snuffling, I'm getting there.'

This threw Ailsa as she wasn't aware she *was* snuffling. However, when the door was thrown open, the snuffler was revealed to be a supremely cute little bundle of fur. A cockapoo, Ailsa thought.

She got a wonderful greeting from the little chocolate brown dog and a relatively enthusiastic one from Sylvia, considering she'd offended her at their last meeting.

'Coco, come on,' she called to the friendly little dog who did as she was told and followed Sylvia into the kitchen, as did Ailsa. A large open fireplace stood at one end and a rough wooden table that had grooves and stains on it was placed under the large window.

'This is the working end.' Sylvia told her, beckoning her further through and then to the right, into what looked like a modern extension. It had windows all along, incorporating French doors which let lots of light in. There were two settees opposite each other in earthy colours, which contrasted with the brightly coloured cushions scattered over them. She recognised the handiwork on one blue and peach coloured one.

'Star?' she asked, pointing to it as she sat opposite Sylvia.

Sylvia laughed. You've been honoured then? She's always been good at needlework.

'Yes, it was an apology that wasn't needed. It will brighten my home up considerably.'

'It does need it,' the woman agreed. 'It was so clinical, like walking into a laboratory. Beautiful, but no soul.'

Two things occurred to Ailsa. One - to her knowledge, she had never invited Sylvia to her home since it was finished and two, this woman was not backwards in coming forward. Rude was one way of putting it. Forthright was probably kinder. She was nearly as rude as Peggy. *Now* she could see the family resemblance between them.

'When...?'

'I asked Ade if I could have a look around. I have a vested interest in all things 'Effie', as you know, so don't blame him.'

I'm not, she thought, I'm blaming you. She decided to let it go.

'You wanted to know about Effie Scritchell and Boaz Haigh. The two are, unfortunately, intertwined as far as history goes. I may have told you I'd written a book on the Witches of Farstone

Moor? No?' she questioned as Ailsa looked vague. 'Were you aware that the witches spread further than the village of Farstone itself?'

'I vaguely remember hearing something of the sort when I was young.' Ailsa replied, dredging up early memories.

'Farstone Moor, you no doubt know, is a vast place, a magical place, famed for the Faestone itself, where the Farstone name came from. The Faestone is the mythical portal to the Faery world, a gateway between their world and ours, only seen by mortals a handful of times – and only by those honoured by the Fae.

'The Fae apparently have the ability to pass into our world through the stone doorway, which, according to legend, changes its location to keep it safe - but woe betide if any mortal should try to pass through to the Faery world. They will be lost forever.

'You ought to read Calum Hythe's book *The Folklore of the Wild Moors.* It has witches, faeries, boggarts, black dogs, the lot. Flora's husband, you may remember?'

'They're married? I thought Flora was called Gardwicke?'

She used to use the name of her adoptive parents growing up – it's a long story - but has taken her mother's name and kept it, not even using her father's name of Peverel. She has done it to honour her mother and the family.'

Ailsa thought for a moment.

'The Fae? Do you really believe in the Fae?' laughed Ailsa, 'I'm only just coming to terms with witches again and then only in a human sort of way.'

Sylvia's eyebrows lifted and one corner of her mouth managed to look disapproving without moving the other corner.

'Do not dismiss anything that you can't prove,' she said.

'Can you prove that they exist?' Ailsa challenged.

'Can you prove that they don't?' countered Sylvia. 'Anyway, Amos is the one you ought to talk to about the Fae.'

Ailsa frowned.

'The Reverend Amos Pennyquick, my husband.'

'Ah' said Ailsa.

'An apology? What did she owe you an apology for?'

Puzzled, Ailsa went back to the conversation of a few minutes ago.

'Star? No, she didn't. She just thought she did. She – you know she's learning how to be a green witch.'

Sylvia smiled.

'I do, but I also think everyone who follows the rules of nature and lives amongst plants, animals and the elements is a green witch, whether they know it or not. It is just following the heartbeat of the earth and responding to it.'

This, to Ailsa, sounded like a very nice way to be a witch. She checked her train of thought swiftly.

'She wanted me to build an altar in a place where I had the strongest feelings.'

'And where was that? asked Sylvia, leaning forward.

'In the round barn. I had such a serene feeling when I first went in. Although the building itself was almost ruined, I felt like it was enveloping me, complete, with the thatch over my head and the ground dry beneath my feet. I felt peaceful. I don't know.... I felt happy.'

Sylvia stared at her for a few moments, then smiled and sat back with a contented sigh.

'What happened then?' she asked.

'I was well, not taking it seriously. I suppose. I'm still not really.' she said, but Sylvia saw that her face said otherwise.

'We chanted some words and then–'

'Yes?'

'It's like I fell asleep, as though I was dreaming very lucidly. I saw two men shaking hands over a bag of gold like pirate pieces of eight.'

'Describe the men.'

'It was just a dream.'

'I'll be the judge of that. Describe them.'

She was nearly as scary as Peggy, too.

'As far as I can remember,' - who was she kidding? They were indelibly stamped on her mind. – 'One had dark bushy eyebrows. I couldn't see him very well, but I think I know who he was. The other was sort of wimpy-looking, like a strong breeze would blow him over. Wispy hair on top, like he was trying to cover a bald patch? Gold-rimmed glasses?'

'Mmm,' said Sylvia. She leaned over to the coffee table between them and fished amongst a pile of magazines, bringing out a leaflet. The Stop the Festival committee leaflet that Lulu, or Ludmilla the vampire, as Ailsa liked to think of her, had been handing out.

'Are you going to this meeting, Ailsa?' she asked.

'I didn't intend to.'

'I think you should.'

And that, Ailsa could see, was a definite plan in Sylvia's mind.

'Now, Effie Scritchell. I will lend you my book. There's a whole chapter on Effie that will give you everything you need, but I can tell you a few things now. For instance, tell me what you think Effie Scritchell looked like, in your imagination.'

I haven't seen a picture of her...' Ailsa began.

'There is only one that I know of, but my research threw up a few contemporary witness descriptions, which tallied. Go ahead. I'm waiting.'

'If I didn't already know you used to be a school teacher, I would now,' said Ailsa, giving the woman opposite her a 'look'. The woman opposite her laughed.

'You haven't answered,' she said.

'Well, in my mind's eye- and I suppose purely because of her name and the poor conditions she must have lived in at Nightowl's Hide - and the descriptions of some of the witches who were put to death at the time...' Ailsa paused, collecting her thoughts. 'I imagine her to be old, bent over, probably with arthritis. Possibly quite ugly and shunned by society. How old? I don't know, they didn't live as long in the 17th century, did they? What, forty? Possibly forty-five? Rheumatism as well from living in a cold, damp building….'

Ailsa looked across and knew from the self-satisfied smile she received that she had got it wrong.

'I'll tell you then, shall I? Effie Scritchell was Miss Euphemia Bothwell, a well-born lady who lived in Bothwell Hall, which was demolished over a century ago but was just up the road from here originally. The descriptions all agreed that she was a young woman in her twenties with curly blonde hair, blue eyes and a pleasing disposition. There is a portrait said to be of her in the Folklore Museum at Weaver's Green. I urge you to go and see it.' There was a moment's pause before she went on. 'That's turned your preconception on its arse, hasn't it?'

Chapter 14

It all seemed to make sense now. Ailsa had wondered why she had started to feel a bond with this scruffy old, wizened witch. The woman had probably been quite a few years younger than Ailsa was now.

'So she'd have been around Stars' age?' Ailsa asked incredulously.

'Younger, possibly. Star has a childishness about her that makes her appear young, but she's almost thirty.'

This threw Ailsa almost as much as the information about Effie had.

'And Scritchell. Why Scritchell and not Bothwell?'

'She was only known as Scritchell from a couple of generations after her death, when all the people from the village who had known and loved her had died. It was because of the folklore surrounding her. Do you know what Scritchell means?

'No idea.'

'Well, if you read the chapter in my book, you'll find out.'

'Oh come on, don't keep me hanging. But the name has stuck?'

'Unfortunately, yes. Now, no one remembers she was a Bothwell and with the ruined hall being finally demolished at the turn of the last century, it's unlikely that they will. My book and the Weaver's Green Folklore Museum are trying to ensure that she is also known by her real name, Euphemia Bothwell. Real names are important.'

'As Peggy has always said.'

'We're Harkers,' said Sylvia as though that name itself had meaning, which no doubt it did around these parts.

'Boaz Haigh - his story is told in the chapter too. I am more concerned with his ancestor, Dinsmore Haigh, at the moment. Your possible nemesis, as Boaz was hers.'

'A direct ancestor? Do you think he's doing this because of a grudge? Because I'm living in the house and on the land that Effie lived on? Or did she?'

Ailsa suddenly looked unsure. If she lived in Bothwell Hall as a titled lady, how could she have lived at the old Cottage?

'I can only reiterate... Read the chapter!' they both said the last words together.

'Coffee?' asked Sylvia and went to put the kettle on when Ailsa nodded. She came back with two mugs and went off again, returning with a very large, thick hardback book, with woodprints of witches, broomsticks and black cats on the cover.

'There are a lot of your ancestors in it,' she said as she handed it over.

Ailsa looked at the encyclopaedia-sized tome in front of her.

'When I have three years to spare, I'll get right down to it.'

'I'm in no rush, as you probably read very slowly, your finger pointing out the words. Anyway, I have other copies if I need them.'

'If you have other copies, did you have to reinforce your bookcases?' Ailsa shot back.

'I had strong steel ones made especially.'

They stopped, looked at each other - and laughed once again in an easy fashion.

Ailsa knew she was going to like this woman. She didn't take herself too seriously - and unbelievably – they shared the same ironic sense of humour. As she had learnt to her cost, not many people did.

'Thank you. I'm really looking forward to reading it now, after you've whetted my appetite.'

'Glad to hear it. I'm also glad to hear you're getting on well with Do–' Sylvia checked herself while raising her eyes to heaven- 'with Star.'

'I am, strangely enough. On first meeting her, I thought she was a bit of an oddball. She still is, but nice oddball though.'

'Agreed.'

'Because I think underneath it all, she is a decent, kind human being.'

'Intelligent too.'

'I've seen glimpses,' said Ailsa hesitantly, still not entirely convinced.

'I taught her at secondary school in Pickering. She was always top of the class in just about every subject. She didn't have any friends, though. I think she'd have swapped all her high grades for the chance to fit in. They called her Dotty at school before she reinvented herself as Star.'

'Why?'

'Because her real name is Dolores Bright. They called her Dotty as a shortened version, but also because that's what she appeared to be. Like a lot of very intelligent people, she's very scatterbrained. Ditzy, I think you'd call it nowadays. She's the equivalent of an absent-minded professor.'

'What does she do? For money, I mean?' For some reason, she hadn't asked Star. She just presumed she didn't work as she always seemed to be at home.

'She could have done anything. Brightest, if you'll excuse the pun, pupil I've ever had. Yet she had no confidence. Nor, as far as I can see, any wish to be rich. She moved from Pickering to her cottage and uses her Master's degree to run undergraduate courses in Modern Language Studies, online, for the Open University.

'She's fluent in French and German. One of the professors runs the occasional face-to-face lectures for her as she hasn't got the confidence to do that, but she's all right online. She makes a living that way and it lets her lead the quiet life she wants outside of it.'

'She has a Master's degree and works as an O.U. tutor?' Ailsa suddenly found all this too wonderful for words and collapsed in laughter.

'I can see you're laughing in delight. If I thought you were laughing *at* her, I'd have to give you a detention.'

'Sorry, teacher. No, I think it's brilliant. Good for Star!'

'She's a happy soul. Happy with her lot.'

'I can see that and I admire it. I don't admire her cat Charm, though,' she murmured under her breath. 'If ever there was a misnomer, that is it.'

'I gather you haven't been accepted by the fussy feline then?'

'Yet? I don't think that day will ever come. You're more likely to find her flying onto my neck, trying to find the jugular.'

Sylvia laughed.

'If you're Star's friend, she'll accept you. I went through the same thing.'

'But, I *am* Star's friend.'

'Not in Charm's eyes, you're not. Not yet.'

'I look forward to that blessed day then, when Charm(less) deigns to accept me.'

They grinned at each other, then Ailsa noticed the time.

'Got to go. I promised I'd see Ade's brother and nephew before lunch. They're just putting the finishing touches to the barn.'

She stood up, disturbing Coco who, it seemed, had quickly adopted Ailsa and had been asleep on her knee. Charm(less) could take a few lessons from her. She thanked Sylvia for the coffee, the book and her time.

'Don't forget to go and see Amos. He won't be in the church now, but he'll be there in the morning until 11:00 a.m.'

'Will do.'

Ailsa went down the front steps, nearly tripping over Coco.

'And you will be at the meeting, won't you?'

Ailsa sighed.

'Is it really necessary?' she whined.

'No, not at all,' smiled Sylvia.

Ailsa walked away a few paces.

'Not if you want to let the Haighs walk all over you without putting up a fight,' added Sylvia in steely tones.

Ailsa turned around and they stared at each other. Ailsa broke first and breathed out slowly.

'I'll see you there,' she said.

'Good girl,' said Sylvia in her best school-ma'am voice.

Chapter 15

Staggering out of The Falcon with a bag of real ale which clinked loudly, announcing the contents to all, she came face to face with Conall, who of course, looked down at the bag then up at her face, smiling his gorgeous smile.

'Can I carry your supplies for you?' he asked, raising his eyebrows.

'They're for the thatchers,' she replied, 'and for casting aspersions on my good character-yes, you can carry them,' and she handed the heavy bag to him.

'I would like to see it completed anyway, 'he said, and the words pleased her.

Wolf loped alongside them as they turned into her driveway and began the long walk to the barn. The weather was turning and the sun had come out. Scanning the grounds, she could see everything bursting into life. The sun made the whole place seem so much better - and look much better too. She had never seen the grounds in the summer months and she was so looking forward to it now.

Between the newly-found warmth of the sun and the walk to the barn, Ailsa found she was sweating by the time she reached the top. She looked at Conall by her side. He was as cool as the proverbial cucumber, even with the weight of the bag.

'Where are you all?' she shouted.

'In your regally-thatched palace, your Majesty,' came Ade's voice from inside. She had a feeling he would be here too and had brought plenty of ale accordingly.

'You needn't kneel, we're not on ceremony today,' she laughed as she entered. The sun had been shining on the new thatch as she approached the barn and she thought it looked magnificent.

The wattle and daub had been repaired and replaced by an elderly man from the next village. A master craftsman, as were the thatchers. For all his advanced years, she had seen the wattle and daub man helping out, and clambering up the thatch with a stook for the others to fix.

Most of the light came from a wide barn door, facing southeast to get the sunlight in the morning. Now, though, she saw that storm lanterns had been placed around the beams in the middle.

'We just thought we'd add a little extra for you,' Ade's brother Niall said, pointing to some stone slabs sunken slightly into the ground in the centre, with hay bales placed further back, around them. 'so you could light a fire here if you wanted.'

Ailsa looked dumbly down at the central fire pit. She didn't say anything, which worried Niall.

'The smoke escapes through the thatch,' he explained.

She looked up and then turned slowly round, taking the whole building in. She still didn't say a word. Niall looked across at Ade, who shrugged. He tried to explain again.

'If we put a hole in for a chimney see,' he was stumbling over his words now, 'it would cause an updraft that might set the thatch on fire and you wouldn't –'

'I love it,' she smiled ecstatically. 'I love every little bit of it, from the beautiful thatch to the new walls - and I can't believe you've made a central fire pit for me. It's perfect, just how I imagined it in the first place.'

There was a collective sigh of relief.

'Well, continued Niall, in a more confident voice. 'Now the pit only needs to be finished off. Stones around it, you know?'

'I just want to tell you all that you have made the most fantastic job of it. More so than I could

136

ever have dreamt of. I am so pleased and you will all be getting bonuses in with your wages.'

'Does that include me?' tried Ade.

'You've already had yours- and that was well deserved too. I can't tell you how–' and here she had to leave off as her voice was breaking up.

Get a grip, woman, she thought to herself as tears threatened to fall. She felt a hand squeeze her shoulder and turn to look into Conall's amber eyes.

'And I believe she's brought you another bonus,' he said, putting the bag down.

They all dived in and brought out the bottles of golden liquid.

'Thrussels golden thatch! Best ale you can get,' said Niall.

'You *would* say that,' laughed Ade.

'You're only jealous cos there isn't a Thrussels Golden Carpenter.'

'One day....' Ade replied.

'Oh, I forgot to bring a bottle opener,' Ailsa apologised.

'No problem for us. Real men open bottles with their teeth.' Ade said.

'That's no good for Ernie,' replied Niall, looking over at the elderly man. 'His teeth will fly out if he tries that.'

There was laughter and general mickey-taking, along with the relief of a job well done.

After Niall's son had produced a Swiss Army knife, they all opened a bottle, including Ailsa - and Conall, who seemed to be accepted as one of them - and clinked them together over the fire pit as they sat on the hay bales. As she took a swig of hers, Ailsa saw Conall looking across to his right. She noticed his gaze had come to rest on the altar that she and Star had set up.

He wandered over to it and after a bit more banter with the lads, she went over to join him.

'It's something Star and I made.'

'An altar,' he said simply.

'Yes, I suppose so.' She felt embarrassed. He bent down and picked up the one object that meant something to her. The piece of wood she had in her hand when she saw her vision. The one that had felt warm in her hand.

He rolled the wood around between his hands, stroking the outer bark with his thumb.

'Can I take this?' he asked suddenly. She felt stricken but couldn't understand why. 'It's all right,' he smiled gently at her and took her hand, 'I'll bring it back, I promise. I just feel that it isn't complete yet.'

She nodded. She trusted him completely and that was definitely a new feeling for her. He reached down for his bottle and held it up in front of him.

138

'To you. Ailsa, for having the gift to realise your dream and to follow your instincts.'

Their bottles met in mid-air, but their eyes were locked on each other's. A feeling that started in the pit of her stomach found its way to her throat and threatened to come out as words she shouldn't say. What was happening to her? She looked at Conall's perfect face, his eyes never leaving hers - and found she didn't care. Whatever it was, it felt good.

*

After christening the barn with Thrussel's Golden Thatch, she felt it appropriate to visit the vicar the next morning. His family had apparently been here for many generations. She was reminded of a saying in the Cold Comfort Farm book and paraphrased it to herself.

'There have always been Pennyquicks in Hatton-le-Hollow.'

She had spent the early part of the morning deciding to add a wall of colour, possibly green, in her sitting room and to buy a couple of colourful throws to go over her tan sofas. There needed to be a few paintings on the ivory walls, too. She knew she had a lot to do to make it hers, but she also knew she would get there.

Sylvia had been right. That newness *was* clinical, but she was working on it. If she kept on

Star's good side, she might receive another colourful cushion cover. Maybe she ought to do something where Star had to apologise again with a knitted gift. She was basing her whole sitting room colour scheme around that one gift.

St. Cedd's church was set near the edge of the village. It was unusual in that it had neither tower nor steeple. Tall trees grew on three sides and it appeared to Ailsa to resemble an old manor house more than a church, if it hadn't been for the open bell tower perched on the top.

She had looked it up when she came to live in the village. It was only built in the early years of the 20th century but was on the site of an earlier chapel. One had to ask, as is usually the case, if there was also an even older pagan site there, which the Christians made use of later.

Pushing open the solid wooden door, which creaked as she did so, she was surprised to find a very plain place of worship inside. Although in one way, she approved of its plainness as she didn't like too many gaudy, ostentatious reminders of the church's wealth that were found in some others.

She walked down to the front. There was an altar table covered with a blue-edged white cloth and behind it were beautiful oak carvings. No sign of the vicar, though. She couldn't see an anteroom, which he might have disappeared into.

'Reverend Pennyquick,' she called out, her voice bouncing off the walls.

She looked at her phone. 10:30 a.m. Had she left it too late and he'd already gone? She played for time in case he came back. She examined the stone font and the organic carving on the wooden lectern. She marvelled at the depiction of St.Cedd in the stained glass window- but no Reverend Pennyquick appeared. Giving up, she went to pull the old door open again and as she reached out, she had to jump backwards to avoid the door, which was being pushed open by the Reverend, complete with a bacon sandwich in his left hand, with the tantalising smell reaching her before he did.

Chapter 16

'Oh my goodness. I'm so sorry, my dear. I didn't think anyone would be here at this time.' He indicated the sandwich. 'I forgot to have breakfast this morning, so a visit to Esme's bakery was in order. Would you like some?'

He made to tear the bread cake in half, but Ailsa stopped him.

'No, thank you anyway. I'm here to pick your brains. Sylvia said I should talk to you.'

'I'd be very glad to talk to you. Come and sit down.'

Taking bites of the bacon sandwich- she would have to get one now on the way home- he led her to one of the plain wooden pews and turned to her expectantly. She suddenly wondered if he thought she wanted his help in a Christian way.

'I'm not here to confess or anything,' she started.

'Good, because we don't do that here, although I'll gladly listen if you want to offload any problems.'

'What Sylvia said was that you would know about Boaz Haigh.'

She kept quiet about the Fae, unsure if Sylvia was having her on.

'Ah, Boaz Haigh, Effie Bothwell's murderer in all but name. Is there anything specific? Sylvia has written a book on it, which will help on that score.'

'I know, she has lent it to me. She just said to visit you.' She decided not to tell him that his wife had mentioned the Fae as well.

'I suppose you know that Dinsmore Haigh is his direct descendant?'

'Your wife told me. So his family have always lived here?'

'There's always been Haighs in Hatton-le-Hollow.' He grinned, his thin, lined face lighting up.

'Cold Comfort Farm!' she laughed. 'I was just thinking of that in relation to you Pennyquicks.'

'That's true. We've lived in and around Hatton-le-Hollow for at least as long as the Haighs. In fact, the Haighs disappear every couple of generations, usually because they've been drummed out of town for misdemeanours. Unfortunately, they tend to

143

return, hence Dinsmore and his wife are in residence at the old farm.'

'Was Boaz drummed out of the village then?'

'More or less, and my ancestor Malachi Pennyquick did the drumming.'

'It doesn't sound as though you're too fond of the Haighs?' she asked.

'One tries not to judge all generations the same because by the law of averages, they can't all be bad.' Ailsa thought of her conversation with Sylvia in the Wildflower Meadow, 'but then another bad one rears its head and upsets your capability for compassion.'

'Dinsmore *is* bad, then? Has he got any decency in him that I could appeal to?'

Amos looked doubtful.

'Possibly not. There does seem to be an evil streak in the family and he is embracing it. We must live in hope that they will find their way back eventually.'

Ailsa pulled a face and Amos caught the look.

'I'm sure he won't stop your plans, Ailsa.'

'Are you? I wish I could be as sure.'

They both sat in silence for a moment before Amos pulled himself together.

'Don't forget to read Sylvia's book. I recommend it.'

'You *would* or you'd be in trouble.'

144

They laughed.

'I see you've got my wife's measure,' he smiled.

Ailsa stood up. She hadn't really learnt anything new, apart from Amos's ancestor being involved. She would go now and not mention anything about the Fae to this obviously religious man.

'And the Fae?' she blurted out. What? How? Sometimes she wasn't sure her mouth belonged to her.

'Sylvia said you were sceptical?'

'Very,' she replied. Of course, they would have talked.

'You don't believe in fairies then?'

'I'd like to reply in the negative but my life was blighted by an early introduction to Peter Pan. I have the same problem as agnostics do. The thing that stops them from being atheists and saying God doesn't exist, is the possibility of being struck down by a thunderbolt, sent from the same God they believe may not exist.'

Amos acknowledged this with a wry smile. 'But your point is? On the fae?'

'Surely you've read Peter Pan?' she asked incredulously.

'Something is stirring in my memory.'

145

'It says – "Every time you say you don't believe in fairies, there's a fairy that falls down dead".'

'Ah, but if you *didn't* believe in them, that would have no meaning.'

'Touche' she said.

They smiled at each other, but then Amos's face grew serious.

'It is a serious thing, really. The Fae *are* disappearing.'

The shock on Ailsa's face must have been apparent to him.

'You can't tell me you believe in them?'

'Of course I do,' he replied straight away. He looked at her confused expression and tried to explain.

'The Fae might not look like our concept of fairies - tiny, delicate little things with paper-thin wings-' Ailsa remembered her own mistaken preconceptions of Effie. 'And they may not sit about on toadstools wearing red pointed hats either, but they do exist. Blame my complete immersion amongst the strong folklore traditions of this district if you like, but I have no doubts.

'They are a race of beings just like we are. They even look almost like us. They are not exactly of this world but are able to move between their world and ours. A truly remarkable race. They are what would be termed an endangered species if the scientists knew. Luckily, their scientific brains don't allow them to see the truth of the natural world or the Fae would be living in laboratory conditions while having experiments conducted on them. I believe the Fae are addressing their possible decline. I'm not sure how.'

He looked at Ailsa, who still wore an expression of disbelief on her face. He continued.

'Everything now is technology, screens, science- with no room left to delve into, not only what *does* exist in the natural world, but what *could* exist there. The stories passed down for hundreds of years about the Fae were not just stories for the majority of people; they really believed in their existence. Of course, there were gross exaggerations in the telling, like all the best stories, but, as with the legend of Robin Hood, there has to be something, way back, that started it all. Possibly even before our race had fully established itself.'

'There's no smoke without fire, in other words,' said Ailsa.

'Exactly that,' the reverend replied.

'I'm not saying I accept what you believe,' she asked, 'but why are they dying out? Not because we don't believe in them?'

'In a way. It's precisely that, or more, perhaps, that they don't fit into this world anymore. They are not accepted as they used to be at earlier stages in our civilisations. They are too different, too other. It has been a gradual decline but a much steeper one in the last century.'

'You sound like you have actually learnt some of this information from the Fae themselves, Amos.'

The vicar opened his mouth, then closed it again.

'I have studied them in a way, I suppose. Look, they are not inherently evil nor particularly good, although they tend to be mostly peaceful. Which is a fair description of our own race, the human race. I have heard that they can do magic of sorts, as they can appear and disappear at will. They also have a great affinity with animals, especially in the wild, as those creatures trust the Fae implicitly.'

His voice faded into the background as her mind travelled back to the images of Conall with the white stag. She came to and saw he was smiling at her benevolently.

'I bet *you've* written a book about it as well?' she chuckled.

'I have. Many years ago now, though. How did you know?'

'An educated guess. Many of the folks around these parts seem to have written books about supernatural goings-on.'

'Ah yes, there are a lot of tales to tell in this part of Yorkshire. It's rife with folklore.'

Ailsa stood up.

'Thank you for your time, Amos. It's been a very enlightening conversation.'

She reached the door but had one last thing to say.

'I'm finding it hard to equate your belief in the supernatural with the fact that you chose to be in the church.'

'Well, what is God but a supernatural being?' he said and Ailsa found she couldn't think of a reply.

*

Back at Nightowl's Hide, Ailsa saw the clouds were threatening rain. Shivering, she lit the wood burner in the sitting room and prepared to walk up first, to where she planned to site a couple of shepherd's huts. They would be hidden amongst the tall shrubs and silver birch trees growing next to the hedge. Each one would be offset and private and would have a view through the trees right up to the top, taking in the round barn and Chanter's Hill behind it.

They would each have a place to sit out, with a fire pit and a barbecue in the treeless parts in front. During the festivals, she wouldn't rent them but would, once they were set up, let her old band use them in return for playing there. They had been good friends for many years and she thought that they would enjoy playing for a small, local audience.

She put her coat back on, went out past her dining table and through the bifolds overlooking the garden. She pulled up the hood as the first drops began to fall. Peering out from under the hood, she was surprised- and not a little annoyed- to find Conall walking towards her. On *her* land. She would have to have words with him before he turned his gaze on her and entranced her, so she could think of nothing but him.

'Hello Ailsa,' he said.

Uh oh, Too late, she thought, her eyes drawn to his.

'I *did* call at the cottage first to bring you something and to ask if I could check on Lilith.' He explained.

'Why? Is she okay?' Ailsa hadn't seen the owl flying since the thatchers had begun or even heard the occasional unholy screech of a female barn owl. She suddenly felt guilty.

'She is well. She is still roosting on Chanter's Hill, high in a hollow trunk.'

'Are you allowed there?' she asked, 'because there's a wall between my land on the hill.

'The hill *is* your land - and the wall has collapsed in places. I simply stepped over it.'

She had seen the gaps but she might have to clamber over rather than step, but she could see that his long... muscular legs... encased in tight.... black jeans... She shook her head and forced her mind back to the subject at hand.

'Didn't you disturb her, going so close?'

'She knows me.'

Again, Ailsa thought of Amos's words regarding creatures of the wild.

'She has not gone back to the barn yet- but when she sees that the activity has lessened, she will go. I believe she divides her roosting time between the roundhouse and Chanter's Hill anyway.'

'I'm glad to hear that I haven't scared her away.' Ailsa smiled.

'Were you going up to the roundhouse?' he asked.

'No, I was going to see where the shepherd's huts would go.'

As soon as the words 'shepherds' huts' were out of her mouth, she immediately felt guilty again.

She could feel herself colouring up, even though there was no way he had noticed her up on the moors near to his *own* shepherd's hut. She babbled to cover her embarrassment.

'I'm going to stop touring as much, keeping it fairly local, mostly. So I wanted a bit of income, as well as the festivals, although I can't see much of a profit at first after I've finished all the work that needs doing on the land and the outbuildings and the car park. Hopefully, later it will be better. Anyway, I've seen a couple of used shepherd's huts…'

Stop saying shepherd's huts, Ailsa!

'… for sale that I can do up and put here- and there - she pointed, but I don't know why really, as I probably won't get permission for them - especially as I might not get permission for my festivals now....'

She took a long, deep breath. She couldn't even remember what she'd been saying herself in her stream of consciousness. Possibly a load of rubbish, which, judging by his expression, was a view that Conall shared.

He nodded, his head tilted slightly to one side, the knowing smile in place.

'I know you were there, Ailsa.'

Could he read her mind?

'But you can't have! You didn't see or acknowledge me. And I wasn't spying, I was just walking.' She was making it worse.

'Should I just say, your presence was felt?'

She looked distraught as though she really *had* been spying on him. Once again, Conall laid a calming hand on her shoulders. He seemed to be pulling her in towards him, almost imperceptibly. She felt her heartbeat quicken and she could feel his breath on her face. Then- suddenly- he was stepping back. He looked confused. So did she. They started walking self-consciously back towards the cottage without a sound.

She stole a glance at him. He looked youthful and for the first time, she realised he was probably much younger than she was. She still thought of herself as being eighteen, but she definitely wasn't.

'How old are you?'

He laughed his quiet laugh.

'One doesn't ask a gentleman his age,' he replied.

'Probably about ten years younger than me, I imagine.'

He frowned.

'I doubt that very much,' he said, reaching up to stroke her cheek, which sent shivers down her spine, 'I'm older than I look.'

153

They reached the gateway and he pulled the metal lever, went through and leaned over the gates.

'This is what I brought you,' he said, and pulled something out of his waistcoat pocket. His long, slender fingers passed it across to her.

'It is carved from the piece of wood on your altar. I also cut off the end to make an amulet. Wear it around your neck for protection.'

'Lilith' she beamed.

There was a perfectly carved effigy of a barn owl lying in her palm. Next to it, a small round pendant, with simple carved lines on it depicting a primitive stag.

'Thank you.' She held them up to her heart. 'I will treasure them both.'

Chapter 17

The rain had continued through the night, hammering on the roof above else 's head. She had originally been sent guidelines for temporary camping sites, space between pitches, water supply, loos, etc., so she had attempted to walk up to the place earlier this morning with a metal tape measure but was driven back by the rain.

Hurrying home, she had found a stone with a perfectly round hole in it. It was behind the outbuilding, which had already been prepared for its transformation into a toilet block. The stone had been hidden in the old herb beds and almost jumped out at her when she pulled out some sage to take back with her.

Star would say that it was meant to be, so Ailsa would put it on the altar with the other things. Not today though. Today, she just wanted to get back to her warm home.

Sitting in front of the wood burner, she made phone calls to her festival guru, who had originally told her the ins and outs of running a small festival. He now gave her a few tips that might bypass some of the rules, if the worst came to the worst.

She had also had a long conversation with Cain, the guitarist with Ashwood, her old band. They had said they would come and support her for her proposed Festival for the Summer Solstice. She now had to say that there was a chance it might not take place.

'We could still have a party at yours,' he said in typical laid-back fashion.

'I'll hold you to that,' she replied, 'and I'll see you in June, whatever. I'll let you know the details as soon as I can.'

The solstice wasn't that far away in real terms and she still had an awful lot to do. A few phone calls later, she made her way into the kitchen diner and had a bowl of soup, looking out at the miserable, wet, grey day outside. Her eyes fell on the doorstep-sized book from Sylvia, and she thought that today was as good a time as any to read Effie's chapter.

She finished her coffee, grabbed the book and went upstairs to her bedroom. The large comfortable room - with its patchwork bedspread inspired both by Star and her own sudden need for colour - was at the back, overlooking her land. Best of all, it had a cushioned window seat and good light, where she had been sitting to read or just looking outside to dream. She opened the chapter she needed.

Miss Euphemia Bothwell.

Under the title was a small, black silhouette of a crone, bent over, gnarled stick in her hand and pointed hat on. The stereotypical witch. She began to read.

*

As you will have learnt, the later concept of witches with pointed hats, flying on broomsticks, their black cat familiars perched behind them, was way off the mark. The previous chapter ended with local witches. Peggy, Devell and Nan Scaife.

Firstly, we see a difference between the woman who takes up this chapter and the earlier wise women or wicca who healed with herbs and natural ways. They were latter-day nurses who had a need to help people. Every village had at least one and they were often old in terms of what old was then. They were usually paid a pittance which the wise women used solely to exist.

Later, mainly in the 19th century, these wise women were replaced by people who called themselves witches, occasionally known as 'witch-haggs' and relied on people's fear of them, as a way of making more money than just the tiny amount the wicca were paid. Many used fraudulent fortune-telling.

Old Nan Scaife used to tell the future, possibly in her 'hovel', and made 'magic cubes' which, amongst other things, included the ground-up bones of a man cut down from the gibbet. Peggy Devell had kept a magic book, covered in strange symbols and travelled around telling fortunes for money. Another local witch, Emma Todd, used a green crystal ball. Perhaps they really had these gifts? Or perhaps they were just outcasts trying to earn a living?

The inclusion of 'witch posts' in domestic homes, such as that in Stang End cottage in Danby, shows that the fear of witches has existed throughout time.

One person who had no pretensions of being a witch was Euphemia Bothwell, or at least she didn't use it to her advantage. She didn't fit into the fortune-telling categories and was nearer in kind to the wise-women healers. Yes, she had a need to help people, to heal them with her herbs and ointments that she made herself. The difference is that Euphemia, or Effie as she was known, did this with no thought of money for her services.

Most importantly, she didn't fit into the stereotype of these women. Even at the time of her death, she was not an old toothless hag but a beautiful young woman in her mid-twenties.

Born into a wealthy family at Bothwell Hall - now demolished, but which once stood on the edge of Hatton-le-Hollow - she had a privileged upbringing.

Her father, who owned most of the land in and around the village, had been a Commander in the Navy and still spent a lot of his time down South in Chatham dockyards in an advisory capacity. He didn't approve of his only child's 'hobby' as he called it and so Effie stopped her mercy visits when he was in residence. When things were desperate for the families, she visited under cover of night so that her father didn't find out.. Her mother supported her as much as she could or at least tried to ignore it, but her final allegiance belonged to her husband.

As Effie had to keep it a secret from her father, she used an old cottage on the Bothwell Hall estate. It had belonged to an estate worker and his family but had been lying empty for some time. It had one downstairs room and a half-room up a ladder, what today would be called a mezzanine. This was probably where the workers slept, using half of the downstairs room to wash and to prepare food and eat, while the other half would probably be used for the one cow they were allowed to keep for themselves.

Now it was empty, Effie set up a table there, on which to make her potions and remedies in secret. A pestle and mortar would have been used and various jars would have been collected for her salves and medicines. A supply of water would have been essential, which she collected from the well on the land behind the cottage.

She seemed quite happy with her life. She had received more than one proposal of marriage, which she had turned down, much to the chagrin of her parents, as, according to contemporary sources, she was 'fair of face with flaxen locks and a mouth that showed much sweetness. Her eyes were gentle, as was her demeanour. She was as dainty and agreeable a damsel as one could wish for'.

She was loved by the poor people of the moorland villages. She covered a distance of many miles on her sturdy hill pony when travelling to widespread farms and often walked four miles in any direction to deliver a salve or a cure for aches and pains- or just to share her company with ill or dying workers or farmers, when she had told them honestly that she could do nothing more for them.

Some people from other villages talked behind her back. Not because they thought she was a *witch, but because of her affinity with animals. She could get the wildest horse to do her bidding, leaving it more docile and manageable when she left. Even wild hawks flew down to rest on her arm when she talked to them. The word was that she had tamed a large barn owl, which came to her call and lived close by her on the estate. In the superstition of the day, a close affinity with wild animals meant you were one of the fairy folk and as dangerous as witches. For the majority, though, especially in her own village, she was a ministering angel.*

The exception to this train of thought was a wealthy farmer who farmed a couple of miles outside the village, by the name of Boaz Haigh. His young daughter had been ill for some time and he had asked Effie to treat her. Effie did her best but had recognised the signs and realised that whatever she did, there would be no improvement.

Contemporary reports suggested that she had told Boaz Haigh that there was nothing more she could do. This was confirmed at the time by the farm manager's wife, who had overheard. Haigh, understandably, didn't want to give up.

As the child's health deteriorated badly, he implored Effie to help. Refusing at first, explaining that she doubted it would make any difference, she let her caring nature come to the fore. She would

161

give her a panacea. If he thought it might help, then it could get him through another week or so of sadness.

The said farmworker's wife was there at the girl's bedside most days. When she asked Effie, 'Will it help Miss?', as even the uneducated woman could see there was no hope, Effie answered,

'It is only honey, peppermint and water. It will help to bring her temperature down a little. I can do no more.'

The woman remembered later, in giving evidence to the local justice on the girl's death, that Effie had also bathed the girl's overheated skin with rosewater to cool her.

The next morning, the girl was found dead. The grief-stricken father – not taking into account all that Effie had done to help – shouted and raged to all that would listen that Euphemia Bothwell had poisoned her. Effie told the villagers, who were aghast on her behalf at these slurs, that he was mourning his daughter and she didn't blame him for saying that. He would come round eventually.

That night, Haigh went to Bothwell Hall and pounded on the door, shouting for Euphemia Bothwell to come out and face him. He held a blunderbuss in his hands and nobody, including the terrified female inhabitants of the Hall, was in any doubt that he would use it.

Eventually, calmed down by his distraught wife, who had followed him, he returned home, but not before hatching a plan.

This was, of course, the time of the witch-hunts. They had mostly been confined to the South, notably Essex and then to East Anglia further North. The earlier witch trials were in Scotland and in Lancashire – the Pendle Witches – but none had yet reached Yorkshire.

The day after his daughter's funeral, a witchfinder hired from Norfolk by Haigh showed up at Bothwell Hall with his men. Elphias Starrock loved his job because the population of the towns and villages paid him well to rid them of any witches they accused. Looking at the meagre collection of houses in this small village of Hatton-le-Hollow, he couldn't see large amounts of money heading his way. No matter, because the local farmer, Boaz Haigh, was paying him well to accuse this woman of witchcraft by causing his daughter's death.

Eventually, after banging on the door with no reply, he gave a curt nod to his men, who burst their way into the Hall, searching the rooms and overturning furniture. After looking in every nook and cranny, there was no sign of the daughter. Her

163

mother said that she had gone to live with a relative down South, as she had been worried about Haigh's violent behaviour, but she couldn't give an address.

Starrock reluctantly had to tell the farmer that she was no longer there and had fled the village. In refusing to pay Starrock, Haigh ruined his chances of getting the witch-finder to return. Convinced that Effie was still here, Haigh made enquiries about any friends or family around these parts who might be hiding her. He had the door slammed in his face wherever he went. He was hated for what he was doing.

The mass hysteria that had swept Scotland for the Berwick witches and England for the Chelmsford witches was now starting to spread through the country again. The fervour with which some townspeople turned on and testified against their innocent, former neighbours was beyond belief and usually started with vindictiveness through some imagined slight or through jealousy..

The villagers of Hatton-le-Hollow, though, knew Effie for what she really was, a caring, compassionate, young woman who had cured many of their own families.

Boaz Haigh instructed his farmworkers to comb the surrounding countryside looking for

164

Effie Bothwell. They reluctantly did this if they wanted to keep their jobs.

Effie, meanwhile, had been in hiding. She hadn't gone down South, there was no time. She had slipped out of the back when Starrock and his men had shown up and had been hiding out in the abandoned farmworkers' cottage on the main street, where she used to make her potions.

She slept on the half-floor upstairs, covering herself with straw. Lilith, her pet barn owl, had been roosting next to her during the day, asleep but still alert to any danger. At night, she flew outside, ready to pounce on anyone who would harm her. She protected her. After two near misses, Effie escaped to the top of the field and hid in one of the animal stores inside the round barn, with Lilith again perched on the rafters by day, and on Chanter's Hill at night, keeping a lookout.

She had been living on herbs and on eggs from the chickens roaming around. There was water from the well behind the cottage for her to drink..

Unfortunately, as she went one day to collect water, Boaz Haigh, on his way home from a search, saw her and gave chase as she raced back up towards the barn. When he caught her, Heaven only knows what he did to her, but she was covered in blood and bruises when he finally marched her into the village. He told his foreman, whom he had found on the street, to go and ride to York to fetch Starrock, whom he knew had been staying there. He had to offer double what he had before.

The only good thing was that Haigh's face was almost unrecognisable. He had been attacked by Lilith. His skin was hanging in strips at the front of his cheek and one of his eyes was bloody and useless. The foreman said later that he had heard unearthly screeches coming from the land behind the cottage just before that and thought all the devils of Hades had been released.

The next evening, Starrock arrived with his men. They had been calling at Farstone to round up some of the women accused of witchcraft there and thought it wasn't too far out of the way for the good money he'd been offered.

He advised Haigh not to involve the villagers, but they would carry out the 'swimming' test in private tonight - and he would bear witness. They would tie her hands and feet and throw her in Hatton Beck, which was in full flow at the moment. If she sank and drowned, she was innocent; if she floated, she was guilty of being a witch and would be taken for trial in York.

Effie was in a severely weakened state, deprived of sleep and food and having undergone whatever mistreatment Haigh had made her go through. She went with them as the day turned in to night and wished for her death to come to put an end to the torment. Almost comatose, she floated to the surface and was grabbed by Starrock, who declared her guilty, then threw her over one of the men's horses and took her to York, after pocketing his blood money.

She was never seen again in Hatton-le-Hollow. People there might have believed Effie's mother's original attempt to put off her daughter's assailants, by thinking she was safe down South, if it hadn't been for a couple of Haigh's farm workers.

They were instructed to tie her up during the 'swimming' and felt so guilty that they went home and told their wives. When Haigh denied this, the foreman who had seen the state of Euphemia Bothwell after Haigh had finished with her finally broke his silence. His guilt had overwhelmed him. He told anyone in the village who would listen, what his thoughts were about the whole business.

The same night that they found out, the villagers rose as one and marched across the fields to Haigh's farm. They dragged him and his wife out of bed, sent them on their way and - to make sure they didn't return- they set fire to the farmhouse.

Effie was sentenced to death by hanging at York but died in York dungeon before she could be executed. By this time, the villagers had already taken their revenge in her name.

Her name lives on in Hatton-le-Hollow. The cottage she hid in for almost a week is still called Nightowl's Hide from her and Lilith's brief sanctuary there. Over time, she became known as Effie Scritchell, referring to the screech owl, which was how it was pronounced around those parts and which came from the unearthly noise the barn owl used as a warning. They had the nickname 'ghost owl' as well, because of the large white form, gliding soundlessly across the night sky. Boaz Haigh said he thought Effie's barn owl, Lilith, was her familiar, but Effie had always had an affinity with birds and animals.

There have been calls for the council to erect a plaque there on the ruins of the Hide, to commemorate Euphemia Bothwell, but nothing has been done, even after years of campaigning.

The remains of the Iron Age barn, which Effie used, still stand at the top of the land. As does Chanter's Hill, where it is rumoured her bones lie and her spirit looks out over the land she loved so much.

Many years later, well after the Bothwells had vacated Bothwell Hall and left it to run to ruin, it is said that her parents commissioned a local stoneworker to carve an effigy of Lilith to stand on the land, still guarding the Hide and the land for Effie.

Chapter 18

Effie Bothwell's story had a profound effect on Ailsa. From having a surfeit of witches around her when she was a child. From being brought up reluctantly with the legend of the Farstone witches. From having venom whispered in her ear by her mother about those' creatures', she found she had become a convert.

Effie was an ordinary woman. No, an *extraordinary* woman. She cared about people and tried to help them, and all it took was one man spouting poisonous lies to the authorities, and her life, which showed such promise, was cut short in a horrific way.

Were Ailsa's own ancestors or those of the people who still lived in Farstone, persecuted for the same thing? For just trying to help people? Even if the relatives knew in their hearts there was no hope for their patient.

She did remember hearing, thinking back, that many of the wise women of Farstone had been rounded up like cattle in the streets and bundled into carts to be taken away for trial.

Had she misjudged them all this time? She knew, more than most people, that the Witches of Farstone, both past and present, were just normal people. Alright, even she had to admit that many of them had unique abilities. Gifts, perhaps, was the right word?

Binky Peverel, as fluffy and absent-minded as she was, could actually see into the future.

Jennet Cayley, nee Gardwicke, had recently found she could read the crystals and interpret them, according to the energy they gave off when held by her or another person.

Flora Gardwicke had no idea of her heritage before she came to Farstone- but already knew that she had an incredible affinity to animals- and her powers of empathy, which were a recent discovery, had become renowned. She could tell what a person was thinking or what the problem or issue was by just holding their hands or looking at them. Ailsa tried not to think about Flora's words, 'we have a bond', when Ailsa had guessed about her pregnancy. Was it a guess? Why would it enter her head? Her mind closed the subject.

171

They were all ordinary people who had a certain gift thrust upon them, or were born with it. It didn't make them scary people. It didn't make them crazy and it didn't make them evil. They didn't deserve the mistrust or the shunning. They didn't ask for any of it. They just used the gift they were given, and all for good as far as she knew.

They didn't deserve to be hunted down and put to death. The words Witch Hunt now mean a vindictive campaign directed against someone considered a threat to society, even if this just means people holding unorthodox views. It didn't make so-called witches people to avoid at all costs. What it did make them was, like Effie, special in one way or another. Affinity to animals, knowledge of the future, empathy and many more disciplines.

The ancient Gardwickes were one of the most powerful families in Farstone, yet the matriarch of the witches still living today was undoubtedly a Harker. Margaret Harker. Peggy.

Peggy was unique. A good friend of Sibyl's, she had no healing powers, even though she helped her friend in the preparation of the herbal remedies from the Wildflower meadow. She had been an able midwife. No one seemed sure of what her gifts were, if any.

Although she could still remember staying at Aunt Philippa's and going down the stairs in her nightgown. Philippa and her mother were arguing. Her mother shouted across at her aunt,

'Peggy knows the Fae. Who's to say she isn't one of them?'

'Don't talk daft Jane, you know she's a Harker. The Harkers have been here since before records began. She's no Fae.'

'But she talks to them, doesn't she?' her mother screamed, 'Only one that can. The Fae are monstrous and nightmarish creatures. I'm not having my daughter brought up in this God-forsaken place.'

'Found God, have you, Jane? The only holy spirit you've found is from a bottle behind this bar.'

'I wouldn't drink as much if I didn't live in a village of evil witches hell bent on destroying me.'

'Evil? How come we are evil all of a sudden? Why? How? And the only person destroying you is you, yourself. Don't think I don't know about all the stuff you take.'

Ailsa had gone back upstairs at this point, frightened by the venom in her mother's voice. They had left the village soon after that. Ailsa hadn't realised the significance of the 'stuff' mentioned by Philippa, but apparently, as she

173

found out later, her mother had been hooked on Valium, which gave her delusions, including a persecution complex.

She was only now fitting all this together and realising that what she thought was true through her mother's eyes, was false. There was nothing wrong with witches. Indeed, if you embraced them and accepted them, they had a lot to offer. Black witches and Satanism were another thing entirely but as she had never come across this in her life, she dismissed it. She had enough to worry about without that.

*

It was the night of the 'Let's get rid of this incomer with her stupid ideas' meeting in the Village Hall. Both Sylvia and Star had said Ailsa ought to be there, but they didn't know the side of her that would rip Dinsmore Haigh to shreds, verbally, given the chance - and Lulu too as an encore. She might be safer staying well out of the way. She was mild-mannered Bruce Banner ninety-five per cent of the time but the Incredible Hulk occasionally managed to get through, when the unfairness of life poked its head above the parapet. Tonight's meeting might just be one of those instances. The Haighs, especially after she had read about Boaz Haigh, definitely wouldn't like her when she was angry.

The rain had stopped, leaving everything dripping, damp and depressing. Putting the kettle on in her kitchen, she heard clattering on the other side of her fence. Star, putting something in her bins. Pulling on her coat, she dashed out in need of human interaction.

'Star,' she shouted.

A moment later, the tousled head appeared over the fence, a happy grin on its face.

'Ailsa!' she said, 'Are you getting ready for the meeting tonight?'

Ailsa scowled.

'I'm not going.'

'Possibly a mistake, but who am I to judge?'

'I wondered if you wanted to come over for a coffee or a cup of tea?'

There was a pause.

'You can bring your own herbal tea if you must.'

'I'll be there in a sec,' said the disembodied voice as she climbed back down from the box.

The next minute, Star appeared at Ailsa's side door and, taking her muddy shoes off, came into the kitchen. She noticed Charm(less) waiting outside.

'Does your cat want to come in?' she offered against her better judgement.

175

'No, she won't come in, she doesn't like you,' replied Star happily.

The feeling is entirely mutual, thought Ailsa as she shut the door on the cat and spitefully hoped for another downpour of rain. Bringing the unknown mug of tea over to Star, she took her coat off to hang in the hall. Something banged against her leg and she took the stone out of her pocket. The stone with the perfectly round hole in it.

'Oh, you found a Hagstone? Also known as an Adder Stone or Witch Stone. You're supposed to be able to recognise a witch if you peer through the hole. Around these parts, though, they are usually called Fairy stones. We say if you look through the hole, you will see a fairy. It acts as a visual portal into the realm of the Fae.'

'Okay' said Ailsa with a dismissive smile. She would like to believe, but after nearly half a lifetime of being a non-believer, these things would take time.

'Are you going to put it on the altar?'

'Yes' she replied.

Star's face changed and she huffed and puffed for a few seconds. She wore her emotions quite openly on her face. She would never make a poker player.

'What?' Ailsa asked.

'That was quite strange, what you saw in your vision in the roundhouse, wasn't it? Almost like magic.'

It was Ailsa's turn to huff and puff. She may be coming around to accepting the concept of witches, but it didn't mean she wanted to join their ranks.

'A load of rubbish,' she said, 'pure auto-suggestion..'

'Is that what you think?'

'Yes'

A slight pause from Star.

'Okay,' she said with equanimity, making Ailsa feel like a young child who had just been handed the dunce's hat.

Chapter 19

The Village Hall was a long, one-storey building with a red-tiled roof. All the windows were to the left of the large main entrance and it was in front of these doors that Ailsa paused to take a few deep breaths. What was she even doing here? This meeting was for people who objected to her mini-festival plans. She would only come away seething or upset, or stressed, or possibly all three. Still, it was better to see who the enemy was. She opened the door and walked in.

She slipped deftly into a chair on the back row, hoping not to be noticed. Fat chance as she saw Star on the second row to the front, turn around and give her a wave and a huge grin. She contemplated going straight back out. There was one thing, *she* wouldn't be against the idea. Star's innate truthfulness would have made her tell Ailsa if she was here to complain about the festival. She had already said she was in favour anyway.

On the front row were the Reverend Pennyquick and his niece, Esme. She knew there was no love lost between the Haighs and the Pennyquicks, so she was fairly sure they were here just to observe. Hopefully.

There were a few other people dotted about the hall whom she felt less sure of. Stan and his wife from the pub. She thought she could rely on him to back her, though. The man from the general store was there and he always seemed friendly enough. A few others whom she had passed the time of day with, but had no idea what they were really thinking.

Her eyes drifted over to the stage. There were four chairs set out there, with three occupied. One by a rotund and happy-looking man, but appearances could be deceptive. Another by a woman with blonde bobbed hair and a pleasant expression. The third seat was occupied by a mousey-looking man in a blue shiny suit. His hair was wispy and he, too, looked familiar, but she couldn't bring him to mind. Perhaps she had met him at one of the earlier planning meetings she had attended?

Then, the man who was standing next to him- and whom she recognised now from the newspaper photo as Dinsmore Haigh- bent down to whisper something to the man. Ailsa stopped breathing for a few seconds. The grim features, the dark bushy eyebrows coming threateningly close to the other man, who seemed to cower... This was the exact scene that had appeared to her at the round barn altar. No bag of pirate gold on a desk between them, but the inference on that was clear. Haigh either held something over the man where money might be an issue, or money was being exchanged in return for favours.

She gasped audibly and then felt someone slipping into the chair next to hers.

'Recognise this, do you?' Sylvia smiled serenely at her.

Of course, she had told her of the vision and she had seemed to recognise the other man's description at the time, but had said nothing. She must now have seen the quiet exchange between the two men and recognised it at the same time as Ailsa had.

Ailsa nodded mutely and could do no more as Haigh took his seat and the mousey man stood up.

'Good evening,' he said, as everyone strained to hear his weak voice.

'My name is Councillor Gregory Peart. I'm the chairman of the local planning committee and we are here to discuss the objection raised over the holding of music festivals in the grounds of Nightowl's Hide, Main Street, Hatton-le-Hollow, being the property of Miss Ailsa Reed, also known as McKendry.

'The festivals had already been granted a TEN - Temporary Events Notice - for the event originally applied for, as we had no objections from neighbours. However, we have now received an objection from Mr. Dinsmore Haigh of Grange Holme Farm in the parish of Hatton-le-Hollow. We are obliged to carefully consider this objection as Mr. Haigh's land borders that of Miss McKendry's.'

There was a little murmur from the audience and a loud 'tut' from Sylvia.

'If the objection is upheld, then the TEN licence can be revoked, even up to twenty-four hours before the event itself. The potential date for this event is in late June. I will now let Mr. Haigh outline his objections. Thank you.'

Dinsmore Haigh stood up, his tall, overbearing figure surveying his captive audience. His beady black eyes seemed to send waves of hate from under equally black caterpillar eyebrows. His mouth was fleshy, the lips red and wet as though saliva was about to drip from them. He glanced to his left at someone in the front row, and Ailsa now recognised the back view of Lulu, sitting there with her hair swept up into a coiffured pleat.

'I'm raising an objection - as no one else around here has seen fit to - because Hatton-le-Hollow is a quiet village and I want to keep it that way. Having loud music blaring from speakers all over the damn place is going to disturb everyone, especially if the wind is in the wrong direction. Nobody wants these music festivals here, attracting all undesirable, drunken and drug-addled dropouts to the place. I'm the only one with the guts to speak out.'

Stan put his hand up. Gregory Peart asked,

'You have something to say, Mister...?'

Stan Wendell, landlord of The Falcon, RIGHT NEXT DOOR to Nightowl's Hide, and I have no objection.' he said with emphasis, 'Besides, your farm is at least two miles away, Haigh.'

Haigh glowered as Stan sat back down.

'Yes, and it's easy to see why *you* don't object -because it'll bring this in, won't it?' And he mimicked collecting money with his hands. 'Very profitable for you, no doubt. As for the two miles, my land goes right up to the boundary of her land and I keep sheep on that land. They will be affected by the noise and they may be stillbirths because of it.'

' In June?' Esme Pennyquick stood up. 'Not as many in lamb at that time of year. Hardly any of the breed you use, especially. Besides that, you still have many acres of land and other fields you can move the sheep into for that short time, it's only a couple of days.'

'Why should I, just to suit a city dweller who thinks she's a country woman? A witch born in Farstone who's now moved to another witch's house in our village. This is where the rot sets in.'

'Ah,' said the Reverend Pennyquick, standing up, 'Now we come to the crux of the matter. The real reason you objected in the first place. You're objecting to something that is confined to history, the bad blood between the Haighs and the Bothwells, the former owners of that land.'

Gregory Peart stood up.

'I'm sure I, and my colleagues here,' he gestured at the two confused-looking people in the chairs next to him, 'haven't got a clue about any of this. Can we confine ourselves to the matter in hand?'

'You and your pious ancestors,' Haigh shouted, pointing at Amos and ignoring Peart, 'have been a thorn in the arse end of the Haighs for too long. Get off my case, Pennyquick.'

Now Sylvia rose, stately and unruffled.

183

'You said your land backs onto Miss McKendry's land. Not exactly, not the festival land anyway. You are forgetting that Chanter's Hill, which belongs to her too, is between you and the festival – and you can't graze sheep there.'

'Chanter's Hill doesn't belong to her,' he shouted, pointing his finger towards Ailsa.

'Historically, it does. Your great-grandfather had it made, illegally, I may say, into a no-man's land and, as there was no one living there to challenge it, it has stood. Yet now there is a new owner and she will be starting legal procedures to have it recognised as her land once again.'

This was news to Ailsa, who was having to grip the sides of her chair in a bid to keep her temper. Sylvia had done the impossible, she had made Haigh even angrier. Ailsa looked at him now, spluttering spittle everywhere, with his face so red that she thought his head might explode any minute and solve all their problems in one go.

'THAT PLACE!.A place of pure evil where unspeakable things have happened. You'll take it back over my dead body. You've heard of my plans to raze it to the ground, haven't you?'

Sylvia had.

'Well, the witch isn't taking the witch's hill back, I'll tell you now.' His lips drew back in a grotesque parody of a smile.

184

Ailsa had a brief flash of him twirling a black moustache as a pantomime villain. The other man on the stage told Peart that it was all getting out of hand. Peart clapped his hands ineffectually.

It was time for Ailsa to take action.

She stood up slowly, remembering her gentle father's words. 'If you have to shout, you've lost the battle.'

'Mr. Peart. May I be allowed to speak, please?' Her voice was strong, carrying to the stage easily. Peart stopped trying to get Haigh to cease talking and turned to her.

'Miss McKendry, I presume.' He had seen Haigh pointing at her. 'Yes, please do. If you could sit down for a minute or two. Mr. Haigh?' he smiled obsequiously.

'I'll stand,' thundered Haigh.

'Firstly,' began Ailsa, 'yes, I come from Farstone, but that doesn't mean to say I'm a witch, just like Effie Bothwell wasn't a witch. I'm not sure you even know the proper meaning of the word, Mr. Haigh.

Secondly, and more to the point, I think you have a very twisted idea of the noise levels of this small festival, which would not go on after 10 pm. It would mostly be acoustic anyway and I would have difficulty hearing it from Nightowl's Cottage, let alone in your farm two miles away. Much of it throughout the day will be acoustic too and couldn't possibly upset even *your* special sheep with their ultra-bionic super-hearing.

'There will only be a relatively small audience as we are abiding by the TEN rules and we never intended for any more. It will be a small and intimate gathering and the local people will have first pick of the tickets. Many of them have already expressed an interest.

'The power for the instruments such as the keyboard, the electric violin and the occasional guitar would be provided by a medium-sized, solar-powered generator with green credentials. The stage will be set two-thirds of the way up my land, so well away from the Main Street and will have the round barn and the contested Chanter's Hill between it, the farm - and any sheep that may not be music lovers.

'As to the direction of the wind, I'm afraid even I can't help with that, but, as all three festivals will be held in months with potentially good weather, I doubt any gales will blow our music over to you so far away.'

'Contested? You *won't* contest the Witches' Hill. I can promise you that.' That horrible leer appeared on Haigh's face again. Had he already set something in motion? 'and you can't say that your caterwauling won't be heard at the far end of the village, screaming obscene lyrics through a microphone.'

It was as if she hadn't spoken. As though he'd closed her mind off to her explanations. The only thing that was on his mind was the hill, not the festival. Not really. That was just an excuse.

'Caterwauling? Obscene lyrics?' said Ailsa over the objections raised by the rest of the audience to Haigh's rant. All three counsellors on stage were trying to calm Haigh down. Gregory Peart had lost control of the meeting.

A loud stentorian voice sounded next to her ear.

'Sit down e*verybody*! Everybody but Haigh sat down as though they were back at school.

'That includes you, Dinsmore Haigh,' said Sylvia, looking over her gold-rimmed glasses at him. Unbelievably, Dinsmore Haigh sat.

'Now, Ailsa, is there anything else you'd like to say before we end this farce of a meeting?'

'No. Thank you,' she answered Sylvia meekly, all the fight gone out of her. Then, she realised that there was something.

'I don't want to *say* anything- but I'd like to sing something.' There were some black mutterings from Haigh's direction. 'To show you that these folk songs are what have been sung since the Middle Ages - and in some form well before that. They were probably performed here in Hatton-le-Hollow, even in recent times, as well as in all the North Yorkshire Moors villages. This is what my caterwauling sounds like.'

She quickly chose a verse and chorus from The Gardener. Her voice, sure and powerful, soared over the heads of the people and up to the rafters. Her sublime vocals, almost two-tone, ranged from high to low with ease. It seemed to hold a spell over everyone as no one moved. As she stopped, suddenly unsure of herself, there was a moment of complete silence until the woman on the committee stood up and clapped.

'Oh,' she said, 'That was so beautiful.'

The man next to her joined in the applause and so did everyone in the audience. Except Haigh, his wife and an uncomfortable-looking Gregory Peart.

'I'm here,' shouted Haigh – his go-to method of communication, obviously, 'not just for myself, but for you, the villagers of this small community. I'm here to speak for you.'

This complete change of style was undoubtedly the speech he had *meant* to make before he lost control. He must have realised that his ranting wasn't gaining him any support.

'N-now,' stuttered Peart. 'I can't take part in any show of hands here, being the chairman of the meeting, I can only cast the deciding vote in the case of any stalemate when the council meet again. So, I wonder, can we have a show of hands, just for the sake of reference? All those against the Temporary Events Notice for the proposed festival, please show your hands.'

Haigh's hand shot up, as did his wife's, who turned around to give Ailsa her most hostile gaze. The man next to Haigh, after a moment's indecision, raised his hand half-heartedly. Peart looked embarrassed, Haigh looked furious.

'And all those in favour' squeaked Peart.

The hands of all the others, including the woman counsellor, were raised as one.

'Hurray!' shouted Star happily as everyone turned to each other and smiled.

Ailsa desperately wanted to quit while she was ahead and turned to go so that she didn't come face to face with Haigh. It was only then that she noticed Conall standing at the back with Wolf sitting quietly by his side.

Chapter 20

Ailsa rushed to open the main door next to Conall. He fell into step beside her.

'Did you put your hand up to support me?' she asked him, incredibly. Of all the things that had gone on tonight, *that* mattered the most?

' Of course. I'll walk to your door.'

'Star?' She turned to find her, not wanting her to be accosted by Haigh and his wife.

'She's with Sylvia and Amos.'

They went on in silence until they were away from the Village Hall.

'It's a burial mound.' Conall said.

'A… burial mound?'

'Chanter's Hill. It's a burial mound.'

'Oh my God. I wondered why the shape was so uniform. How do you know?'

'It's common knowledge around here. There are burial mounds on the moors, too, if you know where to look.'

'So, who is buried there? On Chanters' Hill? Witches? Haigh's obsessed by witches and maybe that's why he hates it?'

'That's probably why he wants to raze it to the ground, trees and all. Sylvia was trying to get a protection order on the trees the last I heard. Yet the burial mound was from long before Effie's time, probably Iron Age, which would fit in with the Iron Age roundhouse on your land. They buried them near to their community.

'There was also talk of Effie's body being brought up from York and buried there too. No one knows how true this is, apart from the marker stone on the top. Sylvia and Peggy believe it, so that's good enough for me.'

This was a lot to take in.

'Just a minute.' She stopped to face him. 'Haigh wants to demolish a *burial mound?* He can't do that!'

'Technically, no, he can't, but most of the burial mounds around the moors haven't got protected status, although they really should have. Ask Sylvia about it. He has half the councillors in this area in his back pocket. So he will find a way.'

'Oh no, he won't!'

Ailsa was determined that he wouldn't destroy the mound, along with the lovely stand of trees that topped it - fitting grave markers for those buried inside.

'And the roundhouse,' she continued, 'what I've been calling a barn. Surely that can't have survived from the Iron Age in the state I found it in when I came here?'

'No, the original roundhouse disappeared long ago- all apart from the foundations and the post holes. There would have originally been a ditch around it, collecting rainwater from the roof. The post holes indicate the size of the roundhouse.'

'So the one on my land, only the foundations were Iron Age?' asked Ailsa.

'Indications are that Effie's father had it built later on the foundations in a possible imitation of what would have been there. It was used as a barn for animals on his farm and Effie would have spent a lot of time there. As we know, she tended the animals, as well as humans.

'It has fallen into disrepair many times since and has been patched up by whichever farmer used the land and barn afterwards until, finally, it was abandoned - until you came along.'

Ailsa thought about this and allowed herself a happy smile.

'And you have rebuilt it faithfully, no doubt helped by the expertise of your craftsman, to represent the original Iron Age roundhouse, whether you knew it or not.'

This praise from Conall made her smile even wider.

'I didn't realise but I was guided by their skills on what to do - but also, it just felt right that it should look like that. The wattle and daub walls, the rafters and most importantly, the thatch. I hope Lilith can still use it? The entrance is high and wide.'

'Don't worry about Lilith. She spends most of her time on Chanter's Hill anyway, protecting the hill and the trees, which makes me think that perhaps Effie *is* buried there?'

'But it's obviously not the same Lilith,' she said.

He smiled at her but said nothing.

'I want to promise them,' she continued, 'both Effie and Lilith, that I won't let any harm come to Chanter's Hill. Do you think that Lilith will be around somewhere there tonight?'

'I'm sure that she will, but go in and try and get some rest. She will know that you will do your best.'

There it was again. As though he could tell what an animal or bird was thinking. Although…

she could tell what Charm(less) was thinking, but that wasn't hard and usually involved disagreeable and unfriendly thoughts. On both sides.

They were standing in front of Nightowl's Hide now. She looked up at him tentatively.

'Would you like to come in for a coffee?'

Did that sound like a come-on?

'Or something alcoholic?'

Did that sound worse? She could feel a flush starting on her cheeks, but his answer saved her.

'No, thank you.' She felt a pang of disappointment. 'I have a way to walk before I get back home.'

The shepherd's hut, of course.

'You can stay here tonight instead if you want? Save you a walk?'

Aargh! No! Why had she blurted that out? Apart from the fact that there were no beds yet in the other bedrooms. Oh God.

He smiled, as though he could read her thoughts.

'It is very kind of you, Ailsa,' her name sounded like silk when he said it, 'but I must get back.'

'Yes,' she said with her head down, turning away. Then she felt strong hands on her shoulders, turning her back.

'But perhaps another time?' he whispered in her ear and slowly brought his lips - kissing her cheek all the way down - onto her lips. How could a kiss be so soft and so gentle- yet so intense, so passionate? He moved her away from him and gazed into her eyes. Bringing his hands up and smoothing her hair on each side of her head, he pulled her into his body. He kissed her again before striding off with Wolf, leaving her staring after him for minutes afterwards, until the trembling stopped.

Chapter 21

A week later, the letter arrived. The council had voted against using land at Nightowl's Hide for festivals and revoked the Temporary Events Notice, previously granted. There was no mention of Ailsa being able to appeal against the decision. In their minds, it was cut and dried. Well, she would disabuse them of that notion.

She decided she was just going to go ahead and get things ready, as though the event was taking place as originally thought. She would have everything finished and vendors and musicians would be told to save the date or be on call. She wouldn't be caught napping, despite their best efforts.

There were only another four weeks until the Solstice festival. She was pushing it time-wise anyway, but she wasn't going to make this an excuse to give up. She had come too far to do that.

She *would* appeal and hope permission came through in time.

The wash house and toilet block for the campers had already started and would be finished in another three weeks. Four loos and four sinks - basic, but it was all that was needed. Campers were a hardy lot.

The Shepherd's Huts could wait until all this council business was out of the way. It wasn't likely that they would grant her permission just now anyway. If the festival did go ahead, she would hire a Portaloo- or possibly two – and hide them in the shrubbery by the right-hand hedge, out of view. Not the prettiest of things, in looks or smell, but a necessary evil. She would get in touch with the suppliers.

If the appeal she was determined to go ahead with didn't work, what would she do then? She'd manage, she supposed. Maybe a bit more touring than she'd like but.... it wasn't about that. After years of touring mainly outdoor venues, she had come to love the smaller, friendlier little festivals because she had got as much pleasure from playing at those as the festival goers obviously had attending them.

Big festivals meant big business and more stress and, even though she earned more money, this wasn't about the money, but about the dream.

She needed to talk to someone and before anyone directed her to Sylvia, as they usually did, she popped into Ailsa's mind unbidden. She rang and invited her over and ten minutes later, Sylvia was there, at the side door, along with Coco, who gave Ailsa an enthusiastic, Tigger-like greeting before going to investigate the kitchen.

Ailsa led Sylvia through to the kitchen diner and they sat at the table in the sun.

'Will Coco be all right?' asked Ailsa anxiously.

Sylvia had opened the back door for her to run around and sniff at her leisure. Ailsa had never owned a dog, living as she had out of suitcases and in flats that didn't allow them.

'She'll be fine. She may look like a chocolate-covered floor mop on legs and behave like a two-year-old child high on sugar, but she's actually very obedient. Watch.'

The little dog who seemed to be having a conversation with the statue of Lilith, was suddenly on high alert and dashed down to the cottage to see what was 'to do'. She rushed over to Ailsa for a fuss and then to Sylvia, who gave her a treat before shooing her off again.

Ailsa looked thoughtful.

'You said you wanted me to keep the stone figure of Lilith?'

'Yes,' replied Sylvia, suspiciously.

'It's just that they're starting to build my garden wall tomorrow and I won't be able to see the statue because of it. Do you think Effie would mind if I moved it into my garden instead?'

Sylvia smiled but gave the matter some thought.

'We're not even sure that that's where it was placed originally or even if it was from Effie's time. It could have been replaced later, to make sure that there was still a memorial to Effie and to Lilith, her constant companion. So, yes, as long as you don't get rid of it or break it in the process, I think it would make a great centrepiece in your garden.'

'So do I,' smiled Ailsa.

'This isn't what you brought me here for, though?'

'No.' Ailsa's lips were a thin line as she handed the letter over the table. Sylvia read it and calmly replaced it in the envelope.

'That's that, is it?' It was less of a question and more of a challenge.

'No it damn well isn't! It doesn't mention that I can appeal, but that's what I intend to do.'

'Good for you - and of course you can appeal. They didn't mention it because they hoped you would give up. They don't know you, do they?' Sylvia smiled.

'I thought you might know how to go about it?'

'I do.' There was a pause. 'Are you free today?'

'Yes.'

'Then, do you fancy a drive into Pickering? The council offices, to be exact. But first, let's draft the written appeal so we can hand it in today.

*

They had dropped Coco off at the church where Amos was busy polishing pews. The little dog jumped into the front pew and remained motionless, as though she were patiently waiting for the reverend to start his sermon.

In twenty minutes, they were in the market town and had parked in the Ropery car park. They made their way to the council offices, but before they could open the door, a familiar figure emerged.

'Hello!' said the woman from the village hall who had applauded her from the stage.

'Hello Pam,' answered Sylvia, to Ailsa's surprise. She obviously knew her.

'Hi, and thank you for your support at the meeting.'

Pam scowled.

'About that, the whole thing was pointless really. The only point it made -and those of us in the know already were aware of this - was that most of the council are scared of Dinsmore Haigh.'

Sylvia nodded in agreement while Ailsa laughed, ironically.

'That's the strong impression I got- apart from your good self, of course,' she said. 'You'll probably know I got a letter refusing to allow the festivals. The question is, what can I do about it?'

'Appeal.'

'But if the council are in his pockets…'

'Not all of them. The committee was split on allowing the festivals to go ahead. It wouldn't have even been that if my colleague, the one at the village meeting, hadn't voted against at the last minute. Of course, Peart got the casting vote and we all knew which way *that* would go. Haigh was in attendance of course. I don't think he's got anything on him- but he's obviously got *some* hold over Peart.

'Are you saying that basically, Haigh is blackmailing half the council?' Ailsa asked.

'Apart from you, Pam, who is as pure as the driven snow,' said Sylvia.

'I can't deny it,' replied. Pam, straight-faced. Then they both burst out laughing.

'Pam Forbes, retired English teacher, from the school where I used to teach.'

'Kindred spirits.' Ailsa grinned knowingly, shaking Pam's outstretched hand.

'It's not just blackmail, it's bungs. Backhanders paid by Haigh. Or through him if anyone else needs to get an unpopular petition pushed through. Corruption is rife and not just here. It's everywhere. It's a disease. I'm running for the mayoral elections to try and get some proper values installed around here.

'I'll vote for you. Pam,' said Ailsa.

Most of them did last time. Guess what happened?' scowled Sylvia.

'More corruption?' asked Ailsa, 'I wondered how an ineffectual little squirt like Peart had been put in charge.'

'He is more or less Haigh's servant. I personally believe that Haigh has been bribing him, so he will never go against Haigh and have his lucrative extra income stopped. Peart is a big part of the problem. Haigh isn't on the council, Peart heads the planning and is ideally placed for pushing things through that shouldn't be allowed and refusing plans that should be okay.'

'I'm just going in there now to lodge an appeal. Is there anything I need to know?'

'Give good reasons for the appeal, lodge it early and keep appealing, even if the first one fails. Do it well. More than anything, you'll need luck, or Divine Providence.'

Pam and Sylvia exchange glances.

'Come on.' Sylvia said and she marched Ailsa into the building.

*

They were made to wait a while in the ante-room. Peart was either phoning Haigh or working up the courage to face them. Eventually, they were allowed through and saw Peart behind a huge desk. He was dwarfed by it and it seemed to diminish him rather than make him look important.

'Now, ladies, how can I help you?' he smiled timorously.

Ailsa threw the letter down on his desk. He scanned it and pushed it back.

'No mention of an appeal? asked Sylvia.

Well, obviously if you did want to lodge an appeal…'

'I do,' Ailsa shot back. 'Thanks for asking. Here is my formal written appeal, listing the reasons why your decision is the wrong one.'

She passed another envelope over.

'We have taken photos of it next to today's newspaper, just in case it gets lost - and I will lodge the same appeal online later today. I am also asking residents of the village to sign a petition in favour of the festivals.

'If that is successful, it will completely negate the earlier single objection. It will show that Haigh didn't object on behalf of the villagers as he falsely stated, but only on behalf of himself, for reasons that don't stand up to scrutiny.'

Gregory Peart looked taken aback at this tirade. He shifted his chair back as though Ailsa was going to grab him by the collar.

'I can't say for certain when this will go through the committee,' he mumbled hesitantly, 'or even if an appeal will be considered.'

Ailsa heard a growl next to her ear.

'It had better be considered, or I think the general public will want to know why. It had better go through soon, as well or we may consider that you are playing for time. The appeal is lodged, well within the time limit. There is no excuse, Peart.'

Sylvia's stentorian tones hit him full in the face and he visibly cowered.

'If this appeal isn't fairly assessed by an impartial committee, then I will have to take it further,' Ailsa said firmly as she turned to leave.

When the two women had nearly reached the door, a small voice came from behind them.

'That sounds almost like a threat,' Peart muttered.

'It wasn't a threat, it was an intention. I will take it to your superiors at the county council and lodge an appeal there.'

'It still sounds like a threat to me,' he replied petulantly. 'Haigh was right, it's almost like a witch's curse.'

'I'm not a witch, Mr. Peart,' she said calmly and started to turn away.

'Hmmf,' came the ineffectual little retort from the man.

She turned back and pointed at him.

'But it's not me you have to worry about, Gregory Peart. The spirit of Effie Scritchell will know that you are in league with the Haighs and she won't like it one bit. I'm not the witch you should be afraid of. Effie Scritchell will have her revenge.'

Peart's face drained of all colour as she marched out of the office and the building, followed by an amazed Sylvia, who caught up with her in the town square outside.

'Where the hell did that come from?' Sylvia asked.

'I have absolutely no idea,' said a stunned Ailsa. Then a smile started to spread across her face.

'But I think I scared the living daylights out of him, don't you?'

205

They linked arms and went off giggling like a couple of school girls.

Chapter 22

Although she was enjoying Sylvia's company more and more and was very glad of her support today, Ailsa declined her invitation to join her and Amos for lunch at the vicarage. Truth be told, the little episode with Peart today had dented her faith both in herself and in her project. It wasn't even that; today was just the culmination of events that had chipped away at her confidence and why she felt like she needed her own company just now.

She called home to change her shoes and had a quick word with the wall builders regarding coping stones across the top, and a word with the washhouse builders, where everything was progressing nicely, and then she made for the moors.

She had entered and left by the front door to avoid Star. Much as she loved her, she couldn't face her cheeriness at the moment. Star would tell her that everything would be all right and the trouble was that, despite Ailsa's apparent bravado, she wasn't sure that everything *would* be all right.

She came to the brow of a hill on the road to Rossdale, then turned to her left onto the footpath over the moors. As she hurried on, she felt the magic of the moors begin to work on her. It was a warm day, the sunshine was filtering through the heat haze, which made the distant moorland hills blend in with the sky. The dust kicked up from the path as she strode along, but gradually, she began to slow her pace.

She pulled her shoulders back and looked around her. There was a ridge in the distance with the silhouette of single trees spaced along the top. The tune from the film Zulu popped into her mind and she smiled. The sky was blue, but the clouds had a yellow tinge because of the haze. It all had an almost soporific effect on her.

She slowed down again, until she was strolling instead of marching. There were some sheep grazing on the land. More than half of them were black sheep, and she found herself wondering if that description fitted her.

She hadn't, possibly because of her mother, thought that she belonged in Farstone when she was a child. Now, after initially embracing Hatton, she wondered if she didn't belong there either. At the moment, she felt she didn't truly belong anywhere. Before she wallowed in self-pity too much, she sat on a stone and took a minute to breathe in the fresh country air.

The heather was starting to come out and by the time of the Summer Solstice, it would be a sea of bright, jewel-like purple. Down the slope to the left of her, a brook idled its way along, negotiating stones and the twists and turns of a natural waterway. The sound of water over stones soothed her.

Above her to the left, the moor continued on its way to the next village, which was nowhere in sight. To her right, she could see the moor gradually fade away and agricultural land take over. Trees formed a wide barrier between the two.

How could anyone not shed their melancholy when faced with the glory of Nature and the peace it brought?

Without knowing why, she made towards the trees. When, after a while, she spied Conall's hut in the distance, she realised that this was why she had come up here in the first place, even if it was subconsciously. He wouldn't be there, would he? Should she find out? She rubbed the bridge of her nose. Hello Conall, she would say, I just happened to be passing....

She should just tell the truth, and the truth was only just dawning on her, that she needed to talk to him. She needed his wisdom. His calmness. She just- let's face it- she just needed to see him.

Ailsa stood outside for a minute or two, listening for any noises and working up the courage to knock on the old door with the peeling paint. She took a deep breath, climbed the steps and, all at once, Conall opened the door with a smile. Oh God, he must have seen her approach and wondered what was taking her so long.

'Conall. Hello,' she said pointlessly. It sounded as though she had just met him in a supermarket somewhere and was passing the time of day.

'What is worrying you?' he asked as he stood back and indicated for her to go inside.

'How do you know something's worrying me?' she frowned.

'Extra sensory perception,' he smiled. She believed him until he laughed.

'Amos said that you and Sylvia were lodging and appeal this morning. Is it that?'

She looked around her. Two padded, red velvet seats were opposite each other, on top of built-in cupboards. There was a single cast iron stove on one side and a copper bowl for washing up, or even basic washing. She had noticed a water butt outside collecting rainwater.

All across the end of the shepherds' hut- and she tried to keep her eyes away from this- was a wooden bed with a mattress and a green bedspread covering it. The remaining walls were covered with bookshelves filled with old books. Leather with gold prints but more modern ones were there too.

She tore her eyes away and sat on the red plush seat. Conall took the seat opposite and looked at her steadily. He was waiting for her to speak. So she did.

'I feel- I don't know.... I felt very optimistic when I first came here. My dream of a small, outdoor music venue seemed to be on the horizon. There seemed to be a reason as to why I moved to Hatton. It was almost like fate and my future was looking good. I liked the village. I liked my neighbours. I liked the people…'

'Then, what changed?'

'Today.'

'Surely not?'

'Okay. Not just today. It's been a gradual chipping away at my confidence. The objection, the Village Hall meeting, the lodging of the appeal today and seeing Peart. More than anything, it's the realisation that Haigh has everyone that matters

211

under his control. The realisation that, whatever I do, I have neither the money, the morals or the inclination to pay off the planning committee like Haigh has. So the only results will be that it will be a colossal fail for me.

The reason I moved to the village was purely for the music festivals. Although, because I now love the place, I could happily live here without them - I don't see why I should.'

'So you're *not* going to let Haigh ride roughshod over your dreams then?'

'If it was just Haigh, then I would find a way to defeat him, yet we both know I'm facing more than just him. I have half of the planning committee kowtowing to him, so whatever I try to do and whatever appeal I launch, it's going to be useless because of his hold over people.'

'He hasn't got a hold over you though, has he?'

Conall poured her a glass of amber nectar. Whatever it was, it tasted lovely. She began to calm down, although she hadn't mentioned her other worry.

'And, the people of Hatton-le-Hollow. What if they don't want this outsider holding a festival, however small, in the midst of their village? I've really taken a lot for granted and I'm thinking seriously of abandoning it all.'

There was a silence - and Ailsa raised her eyes to meet Conall's.

'I took you for a stronger person than that,' he said, 'one who wouldn't give up her dream because of one embittered man who blames his whole futile existence on what happened in the past. Someone who believes, rightly or wrongly, that he has been cursed, instead of accepting that fact that his farm's failing is his own fault. He has to blame someone else and, because Euphemia Bothwell had no direct descendants, he blames the person who has made Effie's home, *her* home, who has made Effie's land, *her* land.

'More importantly, she can take Chanter's Hill back, away from the no man's land where it has existed for over 100 years, to a place of importance to the history of Hatton-le-Hollow. Chanter's Hill is the mass grave of the first settlers of the village. That means nothing to Dinsmore Haigh. He thinks that Effie Bothwell's bones are buried there, and he wants them gone because he blames the curse on his family for the bankruptcy he is facing.'

Ailsa's mind was whirling. She couldn't take it all in. The first thing that came to mind was-

'He's almost bankrupt? How can he be? He's paying out huge sums to bribe counsellors to do his bidding.'

'Damage limitation. He's blackmailing large sums from one side of the council, which go into his back pocket to pay out as bribes to the other. I think you say 'robbing Peter to pay Paul'? It's not using any of his capital. He only pays out some of what he earns from blackmail. So what is left, he keeps. If he continues this way, he could claw his way back.'

'Is there room in his back pocket for all the counsellors who have already taken up residence in it? Ailsa asked bitterly. 'What about his wife, the dreadful Lulu? Wasn't she supposed to be rich? I've heard she writes vomit-inducing romantic poetry and self-publishes it, so I doubt she will contribute anything to the coffers.'

'Their marriage has been rocky for a while since she found out he wasn't as well off as she thought. Although she does appear to back him in public. It was not her but Daddy who was rich- but he lost all his money on stocks and shares.'

'How?'

'A barrage of bad tips from his son-in-law, whom he disowned, along with his daughter. It was three months before he died, so there was no chance to change his will, if they had eventually reconciled, so he left all his estate and capital to the Battersea Dogs and Cats Home.'

Ailsa thought for a minute, but she was still confused. 'Why does he blame me? I'm nothing to do with Effie. I don't believe in curses. I'm not a witch. I didn't know- or care - about him before he started this...' she gasped.

'Witch hunt?' Conall said quietly as she nodded. 'History repeating itself, ' he went on. 'The same thing, played out for centuries. No rhyme or reason to it. Just an inbred hatred for an innocent soul, echoing through time because the family believe she put a curse on them.

'Yet *this* is his curse. *This* is the real curse of the Haighs. *Guilt.* It eats away at them, at each generation. They cannot admit culpability, so they find it easier to blame everyone even remotely connected to the origin of their problems.

'It is easy now to blame you, now that you have bought Nightowl's Hide. You were born in Farstone, an infamous village of witches, past and present. He thinks you are here to do him harm. It has revived the past in his mind.'

Ailsa looked at him with respect. *This* was the reason she had come here today.

'You're not going to believe this, Conall, but I feel sorry for him.'

'That is to your credit and I can understand that. He is a sad man. Yet, you cannot allow him to destroy your dream. You mustn't give up. That isn't you. That isn't the Ailsa I know. You will find a way, I know this. I also know that, in defeating him, you will help him more than you know. Courage, Mon Brave!'

Conall smiled at her and she felt the world shift. He was on her side. Everyone at the Village Hall meeting was on her side. Courage, Mon Brave, indeed. She didn't understand how she could possibly help Haigh by defeating him, as Conall said, but it didn't matter.

'I *will* fight it, Conall. Thank you. I won't give up my dream.' She hesitated. 'I am going to go round every house in the village with a petition to sign. I've been fair. I've made it those For and those Against with no prejudice. I'm- I'm just terrified that they'll reject the idea of the festival. That they'll reject me.'

'You won't know until you try, will you? How do *you* think they will vote?'

She thought for a minute, letting her inner feelings take over.

'I feel quite positive, strangely enough,' she said, surprising herself with this statement. She stood up to leave and Conall saw her to the door.

Go to your roundhouse,' he told her, 'Feel the peace. Connect with Effie and connect with Lilith. They will guide you, but…'

He turned her to face him.

216

'More than anything else, believe in yourself.'

He pulled her towards him and kissed her tenderly, then, standing on the steps, he watched her walk off until, with one last glance over her shoulder, she disappeared from sight.

Chapter 23

The next morning, not too early as she didn't want to make enemies of the late risers, she walked around the village with the hastily concocted petition.

The doors were answered, without fail, with a smiling face and an invitation to come inside. She preceded each signature by saying that there was absolutely no need to sign, and she would completely understand if they didn't.

By lunchtime, she had to go back to print out another sheet for the ones who had been out or at work and by 7:30 p.m. she had collected the signatures of everyone in the village, bar a couple of empty holiday cottages. One person hadn't wanted to sign because they'd already signed the petition at the pub.

Ailsa had no idea about this, so when she went to The Falcon, Stan held up the sheets of paper, filled with signatures. Nearly every visitor who had called there had signed, saying it sounded like a great idea and had left their phone numbers so Ailsa could get in touch to let them know when the first music festival was. It seemed the idea was far more popular than she'd ever dreamt of.

*

Later, Star answered her door to a woman who was beaming from ear to ear. She looked taken aback, as though she didn't recognise her friend and neighbour.

'Are you all right?' she asked, drawing back inside her cottage a little.

Ailsa's smile faded slightly.

'Why wouldn't I be?' she ventured.

'Because you've been turned down by the planning committee for your festivals, and Dinsmore Haigh is in control of them, so you're not likely to make them change their minds? And you're still smiling,' offered Star.

Ailsa blinked twice, opened her mouth, then closed it again. On the second attempt, some sound managed to come out.

'Thank you, Star, for that very succinct summing up of my current situation.' The words were hesitant as though waiting for something else to come to mind. And there it was.

'BUT,' she almost shouted, EVERYONE in the village has signed my petition to say that they are very happy for me to go ahead with the festivals. LOOK!'

Ailsa thrust the clipboard towards her and Star scanned the names. Many of them had even added to it with 'It's good for the village', a 'Looking forward to them' and a 'More power to your elbow, Ailsa.' There was also a 'Stuff Dinsmore Haigh, go for it Ailsa', after one signature and Star was amazed and amused to find the name Amos Pennyquick preceding it. She pointed at it, looked up as Ailsa and they both burst out laughing.

'I've left a space for your signature above Sylvia's.'

She pointed to the blank line and looked at Star, who coloured up.

'Top signature for *me*?' she said in the manner of someone who had won a Nobel prize.

'Of course, you're the most important one.'

Star smiled so widely she resembled one of the Wallace and Gromit figures, then she signed her name with a flourish.

'I signed Dolores Bright in case they wouldn't accept Star.' Yet, she had written Star in brackets after it, too.

'Perfect,' said Ailsa and hugged her.

Star emerged from it a pleasantly pink colour, whilst Charm(less) looked on with a slightly less vicious gaze. It was more of a sarcastic tilt of the head. Ailsa nearly did a double-take.

She went inside and endured another herbal concoction. She would ask Flora or Mary if they would give Star a few tactful lessons on how to make palatable herbal tea.

She told Star about moving Lilith, the stone one, into her garden but said that she could come over and visit it whenever she wanted - a bold statement which Ailsa might regret.

She remembered Sylvia's tome.

'Have you read Effie's chapter in Sylvia's book?' she asked.

'I have. What did you think?'

Ailsa thought back to her feelings after reading it, as she sat on the window seat and gazed over what was Effie's land.

'I felt angry. I felt sad. I felt.... I don't know- like going and punching Dinsmore Haigh because of his ancestor's actions, which sounds ridiculous until you realise that he is now treating me to the modern day equivalent of a Witch Hunt. Above all, I thought what a waste of an innocent life it was.'

Ridiculously, Ailsa felt tears spring to her eyes, but she blinked them back. Star had no such inhibitions and a teardrop from each eye ran down her cheeks.

'And I remember that Sylvia said there was a portrait, said to be of Effie, in the Folklore Museum in Weaver's Green.'

'It is her, I know it is.'

'Will it be open tomorrow?'

'Yes, it is.' Star sat forward expectantly.

'Then, would you like to come with me to have a look around, see the portrait and maybe have some lunch? My treat.'

Star jumped up and hugged Ailsa, nearly strangling her in the process. It was easy to forget that this childlike woman in front of her was an academic. Though she supposed that being clever in certain subjects didn't mean that you couldn't be naive in real life, albeit fun-loving at the same time.'

'I'm guessing that means yes?'

'Yes!' shouted Star.

'Bright and early in the morning, then?'

'No pun intended,' laughed Star, raising her eyebrows.

'No pun even cottoned on to. My mind is in butterfly mode. So much to remember.'

'Just remember me in the morning.'

'How could I ever forget,' laughed Ailsa, as she left for home.

*

After a forty-minute drive over some spectacular moorland scenery with clouds creating light and shade in the sunshine over the emerging heather, they reached Weaver's Green.

It was a large village, certainly larger than Hatton-le-Hollow and it had a lovely feel to it. The church stood out, as did a magnificent inn, The Wykeham Arms, across from it. They continued onto the green where Ailsa parked up in front of a small parade of shops.

Where's this Folklore Museum then?' Ailsa innocently enquired of Star.

'This Folklore Museum isn't open just yet. Why is everyone in such a hurry nowadays?'

The voice came from an elderly woman who had appeared at her shoulder. Ailsa was taken aback and was stung enough to formulate a cutting reply in her head. Luckily, before it reached her lips, the young woman who had accompanied the older, ruder woman from out of a shop jumped in.

'God! So rude! I'm going to apologise on behalf of my aunt. She won't like it, but she will just have to lump it.'

Ailsa couldn't help it, she just burst out laughing. Star looked very uncertain as to what was happening. Luckily, the old harridan twitched her lips and held her hand out to Ailsa.

'Elspeth Wykeham-D'Evreux, founder of the Folklore Museum,' she said with a twinkle in her eye that belied her overbearing manner.

'And I'm Tess D'Evreux and I help to run it.'

The younger woman held her hand out, too.

'Very pleased to meet you both,' said Ailsa warmly, as she suddenly took to these two, despite first appearances with Elspeth, 'and this is Star.'

'I think we've met, haven't we?' asked Tess.

Star looked taken aback.

'Yes, I've been to the museum a few times now.' Star smiled, obviously pleased to be recognised.

'We only open at 11 a.m., even at this time of year. If people are travelling, they'll rarely reach us much before then.' Tess glanced briefly at her aunt. 'There's an excellent cafe two shops along from here, that does wonderful breakfasts...'

Tess waited.

'Or,' Elspeth's sharp tone cut in, 'they could come back home with us and have tea and crumpets in the conservatory.'

Tess smiled and nodded at Ailsa, who realised that the niece knew how to handle her taciturn aunt.

'That would be lovely, if you don't mind? replied. Ailsa.

'Wouldn't have offered if I'd minded, would I? offered Elspeth as the younger ones grinned behind her back,

Elspeth led the way over to an impressive-looking house across the road. Star just looked confused with the situation, but happy to go along with it.

*

Ailsa had just finished hot crumpets, dripping with real butter, which ran between her fingers, and she now sipped on tea out of old-fashioned china cups. The view from the conservatory- large, Victorian-looking and filled with plants that looked like they could take over the world - was spectacular. It looked out over the surrounding moorland without another house in sight.

'So what's the story? Why do you want to see Effie Bothwell's portrait?'

'*Is* it her portrait?' Ailsa couldn't help asking.

'It is. It was spirited away from Bothwell Hall by Haigh's former foreman when Effie's mother died and before the Hall fell into ruins, it was sold to an ancestor of Elspeth's at Rook Hall. It therefore has absolute provenance from the bill of sale. We've had it checked for dates. It was commissioned by Effie's father when she was twenty-one years old and the painting dates from around that time.'

Then Ailsa, with Star interrupting, told the whole story, most of which was obviously already known to Elspeth. After listening to this, Tess stood up.

'I'm going to take you down there now, so you've got twenty minutes before I open up and you can really study the portrait. Afterwards, you can look around at the other exhibits. I think you'll find them interesting, now that I know your origins.'

The word Farstone had escaped from Ailsa, but she felt that Tess understood.

'And I'm not going to charge you,' she added.

'You may not need the money, but have you thought about your poor old aunt?' said Elspeth in an aggrieved fashion.

'I'm sure you'll manage, you poor soul,' Tess addressed her.

'If you don't charge us,' said Ailsa, 'I will leave it as a donation, so it's up to you- but I do appreciate the offer.'

'There's a girl with her head screwed on.' said Elspeth, straight-faced, before her and Tess grinned at each other. This was plainly a bit of regular banter that they both enjoyed. Although she still wouldn't like to get on the wrong side of Elspeth Wykeham D'Evreux.

*

226

After thanking the elderly lady for her hospitality, they left her watering the Triffid plants while they walked across to the museum. Tess directed them towards the portrait, but Star needed no direction.

She marched halfway down the museum, which was small and fairly open plan and stopped abruptly in front of a large, predominantly dark painting. Then she stood back to let Ailsa see it as she herself had viewed it many times before.

Ailsa came to a halt and turned towards the painting. In many ways, it was typical of its time. The background was mostly black with a faint rose glow around the upper torso of the figure on view. This portrait, attributed to Cornelius Johnson, showed a shy young woman with a plain white ruff around her neck. A plain silver necklace with an organic shape hung below it. A flower? A leaf? It brought a half-hidden memory back to Ailsa, which wouldn't reveal itself. It rested on top of a plain blue under-robe. The overdress consisted of a V-necked robe of a muted green/ gold silk. She felt she recognised her somehow. Perhaps from the descriptions she'd heard about.

Ailsa couldn't take her eyes from the girl's face. Her hair, though not blonde as she had supposed, would have been pronounced 'fair' in those days. Her mouth, trying to smile but not quite managing it, had a delicate rose tint. She looked like she didn't want to be there or have her portrait painted at all. She didn't seem the showy sort.

It was her eyes that held Ailsa the most. Beautifully shaped and a cornflower blue, they stared out of the portrait as though pleading with the observer. They couldn't be described as sad, or knowing, or tortured. To most people, it was a perfectly ordinary and attractive portrait. Yet to Ailsa, she felt those eyes were pleading with her personally. Pleading for what?

She felt a burden settle on her shoulders, but at the same time, she felt a kinship with Euphemia Bothwell. One that meant she would try to honour her and, with that, honour all those other women who were falsely accused. She looked at the portrait and made a silent promise.

Chapter 24

On the way back from Weaver's Green, Ailsa and Star had stopped at a roadside inn for lunch. They were making their way through to the beer garden at the back when Ailsa stopped, putting her hand out to prevent Star from going any further.

She had noticed two people at a table ahead of them on their right. They both had their backs to them, facing the sun, but she recognised Boaz and Lulu Haigh anyway. They seem to be in the middle of a heated discussion. Ailsa, not wanting another confrontation, swiftly ushered Star into a small room on the right, where they found they could still hear the raised voices through an open window.

'You're not making us popular in Hatton,' Lulu's affected voice announced.

'Since when have you ever cared about what people there think of us?' came Haig's gruff voice in answer.

'I don't, but it's still unpleasant being given hostile stares by the entire population of the village. I went to get a loaf of bread from Esme Pennyquick's bakery this morning and I could see she was in two minds about serving me, stupid girl.'

'I've told you not to go there or to any of the places in Hatton. We belong there more than anyone and have lived there almost constantly for centuries but we don't have to give any of the villagers our custom or be friendly to them. We're almost the Squires of the village and we should set ourselves apart. People used to look up to us.'

Lulu was sure this wasn't true. Did he think she didn't know the stories or was he trying to kid himself?

'But you hate the place too. I don't know why we don't move to something with more mod cons.'

'It's not a question of the village itself. The farm is my ancestral home and I belong there. Perhaps we can do something to improve the farmhouse?'

He didn't tell his wife that unless he could find some way out of it, they might lose the place. Farming didn't pay like it once did. Although he knew that was an excuse, as he had a gambling habit that made money disappear far more than any problem with income from the farm.

'Besides,' he continued, 'I have a debt to collect for what they did to Boaz Haigh. After the fire, a new farmhouse had to be built, which almost bankrupted his grandson, my direct ancestor. Real Hatton-le-Hollow natives. Ailsa Reed is just an incomer.'

'I thought you said she was Effie Scritchell's descendant?'

' I said she looked like her *and* she's a Farstone witch, so that's enough as far as I'm concerned. They're all the same, in league with the devil. Nothing good will come of that woman taking over Euphemia Bothwell's land.'

'I disliked her on sight. She thinks she is so much better than she is,' said Lulu, who thought *she* was so much better than she was. Certainly better than the villagers of Hatton.

She didn't know why Dinsmore insisted on living in the cold, dark farmhouse. She thought he had money when she married him. In fact, she knew he had, but she never saw much of it. She imagined a locked room with stacks of gold hidden there, with Dinsmore counting it obsessively. Perhaps it was time she moved on to a richer husband who would keep her in the lavish lifestyle to which she could easily become accustomed.

'Anyway,' she added. 'I thought you said she would be leaving.'

'She will, when she realises there's no chance of any festival being held there.'

'But what if the committee votes for–'

'How many times, woman? The committee will vote the way I want them to vote. The fools don't even realise that the ones I'm blackmailing money out of are paying the bungs for the ones who are just greedy, like Peart, for example. Not counting the money people have paid me to get applications through. They know I control the council. I could make a good living this way.' Even as he said this, a voice whispered from his brain, saying 'only if you stop gambling.'

'But they still might go against you?'

Haigh's laugh sounded like an angry bear disturbed in its winter sleep.

'They will never go against me. I am always there, watching them closely to make sure the decisions go my way. They all rely on my silence. I seem to make them nervous. I don't know why?'

The angry bear growl disguised as a laugh reached them through the open window. Star looked incandescent with rage, her fists clenched tightly by her sides.

Ailsa said nothing, but there was one thing. She had no chance of her appeal going through if Haigh was in attendance, casting metaphorical daggers at the trembling committee, all in fear of them in their own way, except for Pam. He'd got one thing wrong, though. Whatever the outcome of the appeal, she wasn't going to move from Nightowl's Hide.

*

Arriving home with an angry Star, who was still spitting feathers when she left her, she walked around to Sylvia's. She needed to make sense of a few things.

Coco was bouncing about on the back of a settee in one of the windows, a happy greeting already on her face. When Sylvia answered the door with an 'oh dear' on seeing her expression, Coco shot out of the room and made such a fuss of Ailsa that it immediately made her feel better. No one who was feeling down in the dumps could avoid feeling happier when confronted with an unconditionally joyous greeting from a dog. They had the knack of welcoming you with such undisguised pleasure, even if you'd only been gone for five minutes.

'Come through and tell me all about it.'

She led her to the same room at the back overlooking the garden, but two minutes later, instead of coffee on the table between them, there stood two very large glasses of white wine. Without even registering, Ailsa picked hers up and drank a third of it.

'That bad is it?' asked Sylvia.

'Worse. I have just overheard Haigh and, even though I know he controls the whole planning committee, if not the whole council, I also know that, if Haigh is casting his evil glances over them as they vote, I have no chance of winning the appeal or any subsequent applications. My dream of musical gatherings celebrating folk songs and folklore on my own land is in tatters.

'So you're giving up?'

'No, I'm not giving up!' Ailsa grumbled, 'But there's one thing. Haigh thinks I will just move away if I don't get the festivals, but he's wrong. I belong here now and, whatever happens in the future, I'm damn well staying put.'

'Good for you, girl,' Sylvia laughed, 'but there's still a chance you will win an appeal.'

'How? What do you want me to do? Put a curse on him? I'm no witch, remember? Besides, it was just an idea, a dream I was chasing- and I'll have others. Something that doesn't require planning permission, possibly,' she smiled wryly.

A moment later, Sylvia's phone rang. She looked serious when she turned it off.

'That was Pam, she's letting us know first, that the date for the appeal is set.'

234

'Oh, good. That was quick! At least we have got the appeal, which wasn't apparent when we left Peart's office.'

'I've got to tell you that the date has been set deliberately. The meeting will be on June 20th, Solstice Eve. The date you were having your first festival.'

Sylvia looked angry. Ailsa was getting used to knockbacks and faced it with stoicism.

'Then I'll have the party instead. No tickets are on sale yet, so it will be just friends, family and my band. Maybe Conall's band, too. I'll cut back on acts, stalls, catering, etc, but essentially, it will be the same- but free.'

'Free? Can you afford that?'

'I'll make sure I can, yes, because it's both a thank you to everyone and a smack in the eye with a wet kipper for Haigh.'

This plan made Ailsa feel a little better. They sat in silence for a moment before Sylvia spoke.

'Dinsmore Haigh is a complex man. Money is what drives him on the surface, but revenge is what drives him from inside.'

'Revenge for what? We're talking many generations ago now. Shouldn't he let go?'

'I believe and so does Amos, that he is trying to break the curse that Effie put on the Haigh family as she left Hatton on her final journey.'

235

'Do you really believe that? How could she curse him?'

'Wouldn't anyone, when they knew they would die - however kind they were, put a curse on the person who had put them through hell and more? According to the legend, and we don't know how true this is, she said, 'A curse on your house, Boaz Haigh'.

'The curse was taken by the Haigh family to mean the House of Haigh. The family itself. She might just as easily have said 'Go to Hell' or something as generic as that. We don't know for sure.'

'It's ridiculous. Effie was a kind person, not a witch. He knew this in his cold heart.'

'Who, really, is just ordinary? Everyone has qualities that lift them above the ordinary, even if other people don't recognise them. We are all extraordinary in our own way. And who said Effie wasn't a witch? Not a crone with warts, a pointed hat and a green face, but someone who had gifts that others didn't have. Don't forget her affinity with animals and her ability to heal, like Sybil and Flora Gardwicke. Faced with death, Effie might have called on those powers? She would never have harmed any person but, perhaps their home...?'

'You're saying that the house was set on fire because of Effie?' Ailsa was desperately *not* wanting Effie to be a witch, just like she didn't want to acknowledge that she may have certain gifts herself.

'The farmhouse was set on fire because of the high regard the people had for Effie. Nothing more. Yet, a few words, interpreted as a curse, can permeate the collective consciousness of a family throughout the generations. Recent generations have felt it just as much as those nearer to the event. If you believe you've been cursed, it will eat away at you and therefore may come true through self-induced suggestion.'

'And Dinsmore. Haigh believes it all?'

'No doubt about it. What's more, he believes that the only way to break the curse is to dig Effie's bones up from Chanter's Hill and move them well away from Hatton-le-Hollow.

'He's sure her remains are buried there, then?'

'Effie's father travelled up to York to see his daughter, arriving minutes before she died. He was full of remorse and brought her body up here to be buried. He wanted her last resting place to be on Bothwell land and- well, there is no reason to believe it wouldn't have been on Chanter's Hill, a place she loved and where her beloved Lilith still waited for her.'

237

'I really hope she was. Although isn't it an Iron Age burial mound?'

'Effie was reputedly buried at the top of the mound and a circle of trees was planted around her grave to protect it, with a stone marking the grave.'

'So it is true then?'

'Without digging it up and disturbing her spirit, we have no proof. Yet I see no reason why not. And perhaps we should just have faith that that *is* her last resting place.'

' But Haigh could have dug it up at any time?'

'Not without a dispute which couldn't be settled by the council he 'owned'. We would have kicked up such a fuss that he'd be in prison now if he'd tried. It would have to go to higher authorities. It's not something he could do in secret either, because he would have to enlist help. The stone is set in the ground and will be extremely heavy. I don't think Lilith would take kindly to the ground being disturbed either. We all know from Effie, what a barn owl can do when it's angry and defending something it cares about.

'Besides, he doesn't own the land. He says it's no man's land, but no one has bought the land since it was Bothwell land. Farmers have used it for grazing as though it were just common land. Chanter's Hill itself hasn't needed to be used at all - for the most part.' Sylvia looked shifty. 'It wouldn't be hard to prove it is still part of your land - because it is.'

Ailsa leant back against the cushions, trying to take it all in. Sylvia was pouring wine into a glass that Ailsa didn't even realise she had emptied.

'That's why he wants ownership over Chanter's Hill? So he can move her remains?'

'Yes, and just when there was the hope, the possibility of getting Chanter's Hill signed over, as the land, cottage and barn had been left to go to rack and ruin - and no one else would want it- you turn up and buy it. Fate, don't you think?'

Fate? Or communication between Sylvia, and Peggy, and then Philippa - and lastly herself? Maybe there was an element of fate in it. Nothing was ordinary here. After finishing her second glass, Ailsa made for the door, walking very deliberately and slowly so she didn't trip over Coco.

'I've got a lot still to do with the organising, even if it is only technically a party. It will be a sort of dry run for a festival, although with my band coming over, perhaps dry is the wrong word.'

'By the way,' asked Sylvia, 'why were you out at Weaver's Green anyway?'

'I just felt like I needed to see what Effie looked like. It would be nice to think it was her portrait. They believe it is, at the museum.'

'It's been authenticated to the early 1600s, so I believe it is. What did you think to her?'

'She looks like your description, lovely, kind, gentle - I almost felt like I recognised her. The hair, the eyes?'

'Strange that,' smiled Sylvia. Ailsa caught the sarcastic tone and frowned.

'What?' she asked.

'Have you looked in a mirror recently?' replied Sylvia. 'Effie's maternal grandmother was a Reed.'

As she walked away, lost in disturbing thoughts, the words 'we are all related' whirled around in her brain.

Chapter 25

Ailsa *was* looking forward to the party. She kept telling herself that. It was going to be on the weekend of the 23rd and 24th, so it was going to be a Midsummer party instead. She would have to wait and see how the Solstice and Midsummer fell in future years to see what should be celebrated on the weekend nearest. The organisation was still all new to her.

Mainly, whichever of the celebrations she decided to go for in the future, what mattered was that they both celebrated the coming of Summer and warm weather. The coming of the sun and fertility for the land. She checked herself. She had said, 'the future years', but there may not be any festival celebrations happening at all. Anyway, she was trying not to let it depress her because she knew she would enjoy the party, but she couldn't help feeling a bit fed up.

241

It was only Haigh and the committee who would be against her, not the villagers and that was a good thing, but still..... Dinsmore Haigh was still ruining lives just as his ancestor Boaz had done and probably various motley Haighs in between them both. Why did people have to be so awful to others?

She had just come back from a walk over the moors, not even in Conall's direction this time, as she didn't want to talk to anyone. She was feeling uncharacteristically sorry for herself and wanted to wallow away from everyone else.

'Solstice Eve tonight,' Star popped up over the fence as Ailsa arrived home. 'I can come round to yours and we can burn candles and celebrate it by ourselves?'

Ailsa felt bad, but she didn't really want company. Despite telling Sylvia, she wasn't giving up - and she wasn't - she still felt she was banging her head against a brick wall called Dinsmore Haigh.

'That's very kind of you, Star,' she said wearily, 'but I'm not good company tonight. I think I'll probably just have a quiet night.'

Star looked reluctant to leave it at that. Eventually, with an uncharacteristic frown on her face, she said,

'Okay then, but you will stay up to midnight to welcome the new day, won't you?'

Ailsa nodded, smiled and went into Nightowl's Hide. She sat first in the sitting room on the window seat, trying and failing to read a book. After taking nearly an hour to read the same chapter, she went to the window seat in her bedroom. She sat there, lost in thought as darkness fell.

*

There was a persistent hammering in Ailsa's brain. She ignored it. It must have been a bad dream. She turned over and checked the alarm clock. 11:35 p.m. it announced in bright green numbers. She had only been in bed for half an hour!

She started to drift off again, thinking of fire pits, flower wreaths and fairies. Bang, bang, bang. Ailsa sat bolt upright in bed, thinking of fiends, felons and fantoms. There it was again- not thunder but someone at the door? At this time of night! She grabbed Conall's protective stag amulet and put it over her head, just in case.

She crept downstairs in a pair of forget-me-not blue silk pyjamas and shouted through the side door.

'Who is it?'

'It's me.'

Very informative. Luckily, she would know Stars' voice anywhere.

'Star? What the hell?' she said as she let what she presumed was Star into the kitchen. She looked... different.

'For heaven's sake! Surely you weren't asleep before midnight on Solstice Eve?'

The incredulous voice that nearly perforated her eardrums didn't sound like Star at all. Ailsa realised it was the first time she had been told off by her in an angry way.

'What? What have I done wrong? Am I not allowed to sleep n–'

'Put this on quickly.'

Ailsa looked at the garment being offered to her then she looked up at Star and realised this was why she looked different. She suddenly came to full awareness. Star was wearing a long grey cloak, the hood almost obscuring her face.

She held up the garment and placed it in Ailsa's hands. It was the same, a long grey cloak with a monk-like hood and lined with a bright emerald green silk. She looked up at Star. Star looked at her.

'Well, put it on!' in un-Star-like fashion. Stunned into action, Ailsa put it on over her pyjamas, thinking, ridiculously, 'blue and green should never be seen except upon a fairy queen'.

244

She put the hood up hesitantly and stared at Star as though she were an alien.

'Good. Come on. We haven't got much time,' Star said, grabbing her arm and herding her towards the door.

'Time for what?' asked Ailsa, but there was no reply. The small figure in front of her was already halfway up the garden. She followed on and when Star stood aside, she opened the gate set in the new wall, which was unlocked anyway. Star handed her something.

'Here, ' she said, 'don't lose it. There's a pocket in your cloak.'

Ailsa fumbled about for a few moments, found the pocket and pushed the object in. It was obviously a candle. They were going to the roundhouse then. Why hadn't Star told her this? Why accept that she wasn't going to celebrate the solstice with her earlier and then drag her out to celebrate at this time of night? She didn't, just at this moment, feel very well disposed towards Star.

She hadn't been sleeping well because of all this Haigh business anyway, but she resented being dragged out to the roundhouse altar for the witching hour. Witching. It followed her around. Witch. Witchcraft. Witching. She let out an ironic laugh. Star turned around and scowled at her.

'You won't be laughing if we don't make it in time. I've been hammering on your door for ten minutes!'

Yikes! Was this the real Star or just an evil twin who had disposed of the nice one and taken her place? They reached the roundhouse - and passed it. Ailsa, confused, called out to Star, who strode on ahead of her on her little legs.

She clambered over the ruined drystone wall and then started to climb upwards, onto Chanter's Hill.

Ailsa stood there amazed until Star issued an urgent 'Come on'. Truth be told, she felt it was wrong to climb up a burial mound with the remains of an Iron Age tribe there. She didn't want to seem disrespectful. It was strange that Star didn't feel the same. She especially didn't want to disturb Effie's bones, if indeed they were there, at the summit of the hill.

Silently, another figure appeared at her side, dressed in the same type of cloak. Sylvia. This was getting stranger by the minute.

'Chanter's Hill is so-called because it was considered a sacred pagan place. Chanters, in this case, were people who chanted spells. Witches, if you like. Tonight we honour them and the bones of earlier ancestors, buried within this hill and we will ask for their help.'

246

Sylvia linked her arm through Ailsa's, which was a good job as she felt very wobbly, as though this was all a dream.

The soft grass beneath her bare feet felt very real. The breeze on her face commanded her attention. The rustle of the circle of trees played around her ears. She looked up as they stood underneath them. Through their gently waving branches, the full moon was visible, lending its ethereal light to the ground within the circle.

That ground, Ailsa was astonished to see, was not empty. There were figures there, cloaked as she was. She started trembling. Not through fear but from the awareness that something significant was happening here tonight. She could feel Sylvia squeeze her arm and she was glad of it.

Suddenly, she was standing by herself.

'Come forward, Ailsa Reed.'

The commanding voice had to be obeyed because she would recognise it anywhere. Peggy Harker. Peggy held her arm out and Ailsa went and stood next to her.

She saw that she and the other figures were in a circle, an inner circle, mirroring the trees around them. A tall, leafy, natural and protective circle around their human one. The hooded person with Peggy's voice said,

'Candle.'

With only a moment's hesitation, Ailsa pulled the candle from her pocket and held it in front of her, like the others did. Starting with Peggy, the black candles were lit one by one, from left to right, until at last, ending with herself, there were nine candles.

Nine. Ailsa saw the faces of the nine illuminated and slightly distorted by the flickering candlelight, but still fully recognisable. To her right was Peggy. Next to her were Flora, Philippa and Mary. Then she could see Binky and Jennet. Next to them was Star - and then Sylvia. Sylvia had been a surprise, but it really shouldn't have been, she thought.

As one, with Sylvia guiding Ailsa forward, all the cloaked figures set their black candles in holders placed on a large round mirror, which was in turn, set on a large flat stone in the centre. There was a sudden flare of light as the candles reflected through the mirror, illuminating both the figures and the dark branches above them. The trees, already radiating silver from the moonlight, now glowed with a golden luminescence, at once both eerie and breathtaking.

The emerald green lining of the cloaks sparkled in the shimmering lights, which also showed a still, white figure perched in the branches above their heads. Lilith.

They all stood back again as Peggy drew the outline of a circle, sunwise, with a wooden staff, then the women all stepped inside the circle. Ailsa did everything that they did. Despite her scepticism, she found herself fascinated.

They all raised their faces to the moon, the light now falling on more recognisable features without the strong shadow of the candles. It seemed to Ailsa that, with the energy between them all, they could draw down the moon. Peggy seemed to be saying something to herself, after which they all held hands, so completing the circle. Peggy's voice came loud and strong.

'We are nine. Three times three. As such, we call and invoke the spirit of our ancestors. We ask for protection for Ailsa Reed and her land. We ask for protection for Chanter's Hill, for Euphemia's resting place and that of our ancestors.'

She threw her head back, her eyes closed.

Let evil deeds against this land,
Be thrown back against the hand
That caused the suffering, present and past
And this end, our spell we cast.
Let it be done, with harm to none.
So mote it be.

After each line, the others repeated Peggy's words. Then there was silence. Ailsa saw they were all turned towards her. Why? What did they expect of her?

'This must come from you, Ailsa.'

The voice sounded close to her ear, but she couldn't tell in what direction. It seemed distorted. A whispering. The rustling of the leaves enveloped her, she felt the branches reaching down to encase her body. The candles on the stone had fused into one flame, which flew upwards and into her mind. The ground beneath her feet held her close and energised her. She was alone, yet felt the presence of hundreds of others. She began to speak, her voice sounding strange as it echoed around her.

For all the evil and all the pain
That thou hast caused here once again.
I send thee fire and flood and wind
So shall ye know that thou hast sinned.
What thee and thine brought down on me
Will be returned, yet three times three
I turn the tables to thee and thine, thrice.
For our suffering, thou must pay the price.
This is my will.
So mote it be.

Other, distorted voices joined in the last four words, reaching her and pulling her back.

Suddenly, a crack of thunder that sounded like the world was coming to an end reverberated through the trees. Ailsa came fully to her senses just as a blinding flash of lightning lit up the sky around them. She started trembling. Was this her? The words of the spell she had chanted began to come back to her. She looked wildly at Peggy.

'Did I cause this? Is this a bad omen?'

'It is more than possible that you did,' Peggy said calmly, 'and, no, it isn't. It could be that your wish has been granted.'

A moment later, with clouds looming in and covering the moon, the rain began to fall. Within twenty seconds, it went from large drops landing on their hoods, to a cloudburst, soaking them all to the skin.

Ailsa turned to go back home, but Sylvia stopped her. Peggy went round behind them again to the outer circle with the wooden staff, so releasing the circle, and they all turned to hurry back to somewhere dry. She watched as two people accompanied Star, and yet more accompanied Sylvia, all making their hurried way towards the village. It all made sense now. Star not wanting to use her cottage for the Solstice Blessing as she would normally, instead asking to come to hers. Sylvia having 'visitors' staying at the Vicarage. She stood there, watching them and feeling strangely abandoned by them all. She could have joined them, though. So why was she still here?

251

She realised that one of the figures had stopped at the edge of the trees on the way back. Was that Peggy? She was staring intently at Ailsa. No, not at her. She was looking past her to something behind her shoulder. Peggy appeared to bow her head, her hood covering her face. Then she stood upright and went towards the village.

Ailsa hardly dared turn around. The rain was coming down in sheets now, but here she stood, in the open centre of the circle of trees. Very slowly and very fearfully, she turned around. Her heart leapt, yet not with fear. Emerging from the circle of trees was the white stag.

She held her breath for the beauty was so stunning. The whiteness of the majestic creature in front of her was magnified many times. She thought it was from the light of the moon but, of course, the moon had disappeared behind the storm clouds. The luminescence came from the stag itself. She didn't need Peggy to tell her that this was a good omen. She knew instinctively. She knew that they had all been favoured by its presence.

She felt tears spring to her eyes and, remembering Peggy's action, she slowly and reverently bowed her head towards the stag. Unbelievably, in return, the stag bowed its own head before turning and heading slowly back through the trees, away from Chanter's Hill. The tears now flooded down Ailsa's cheeks unchecked, competing with the rain. She felt humbled and incredibly blessed. She still couldn't move.

Out of the corner of her eye, she saw a figure emerging from the trees, the outline obscured by a curtain of rain. She should have been scared. Her survival instincts should have kicked in, making her run for her life, but somehow, she knew she was safe.

The figure walked up to her, reached out and pulled her cloak firmly around her and pushed his own hood back. Conall. She smiled, as though it was inevitable. He took her hand and they both made their way towards Nightowl's Hide. Something in the darkness moved swiftly at their side, keeping pace with them. Wolf.

As they reached the gate in the wall, there was a Shhh sound as a white ghostly shape flew onto the top of the wall, looking down at them. Conall saluted Lilith and so Ailsa did the same, feeling in awe of her beauty.

When they reached the door, the bedraggled figures hesitated only for an instant before they entered the cottage. Followed closely by a wolf-like creature in want of a dry, warm place to sleep.

Chapter 26

Ailsa woke late and stumbled out of bed. She pulled the curtains aside. Pools of water were gathered on the courtyard below her bedroom. Watching lazily, eyes half shut, she registered the hypnotic effect of the last few drops of rain in the puddles and contemplated climbing back into bed.

Her eyes suddenly flew open wide. Last night! Then she frowned, had it all been a dream? Then she remembered something else…but Conall wasn't here, was he? Momentarily disappointed that *that* might have been a dream too, it came back to her that he said he let Wolf run free on the moors very early every morning before any walkers came.

Was that the only reason he had left her? She ran downstairs, but it was all empty. No, wait, there was a pot of coffee on the stove. She felt it, it was hot. There was a clean mug nearby and another one washed up next to the sink. She hadn't dreamt it then, so she can't have dreamt the rest either.

The coven on Chanter's Hill on Solstice Eve. Last night. Ailsa squeezed her eyes tightly together. If someone had said a year ago that she would have been standing, cloaked and hooded and under a full moon, chanting spells for revenge on her enemies, she would have thought they were crazy. Maybe it was *her* that was crazy.

She had felt that same trance-like feeling come over her that she had felt with Star in Lilith's barn. She tried to recall the words she had used, but only the odd one or two came back. Was it a curse? Surely not. None of the - she wanted to say witches- she would *have* to say witches, what else could they be - were bad women. They wouldn't want to hurt anyone, just as Effie hadn't wanted to hurt anyone either.

The words flood, fire and wind had been mentioned. She hoped it wasn't fire; that was a horrible thing to wish on anyone. Maybe flood- that way it would be Karma rather than curse because of the way Boaz had almost drowned Effie. She shook her head. What was she thinking? Curses, karma, covens? This was madness- and anyway, wouldn't that make her a witch too?

She had an awful feeling that one day soon, she would have to think about the acceptance of her heritage. For now, though, she would put it to the back of her mind and just think of last night as a harmless, if slightly surreal, Solstice Eve celebration.

Then her thoughts turn to what happened after the celebration. If it hadn't been for the coffee pot, she'd have thought she'd had a particularly nice fantasy about that, too. She took her coffee over to the table, thinking about Conall. Was she a scarlet woman? It wasn't something that could ever have been used to describe her before. Maybe moving here was bad for her morals. From the memories that were coming back from when they both returned here, it was worth it. She hoped that he felt the same.

She stopped as she reached the table. There, in the glass vase from her shelf, was a bunch of wildflowers. Ones that she recognised from her own garden. They still had drops of rain on the leaves. Conall must have been out to collect them for her this morning before he went. The gesture spoke volumes. She stifled a happy sob and put her hand to her heart as a silent salute to him. Then she sat and drank her coffee, smiling happily.

*

After a shower and a change into cropped jeans and a vest- the storm seemed to have made it hotter but not as muggy- she went down to make

256

more plans in her notebook, while staring at the wild flowers with a soppy look on her face. There was a knock at the door, which she recognised as Star's.

'Come in, it's unlocked,' she shouted.

The next minute, a very quiet and subdued Star appeared in front of her.

'I'm sorry–' she began.

'Oh, for heaven's sake, Star, stop apologising. As far as I can see, you never do anything to apologise for.'

Just then, another memory hit her between the eyes and she turned around to face her full-on.

'Oh- apart from being incredibly bossy last night and shouting at me like I was a wayward child.'

This was said with a grin on Ailsa's face and nobody could be upset by it. Except Star. She crumpled visibly and the tears, seemingly ever present and just waiting to overflow at any perceived slight or even a compliment, were threatening again.

'I didn't mean it. It was because...'

'Oh dear Star, I didn't mean it as a rebuke. It was just so out of character, it threw me.'

'Please let me finish,' gabbled Star. 'I can tell you now, but I couldn't tell you beforehand.'

'Tell me what?'

257

'That it was my first time as a proper witch!'

Despite moist eyes, Star was now looking excited.

'It's the first time I've been allowed at a gathering, Sylvia thought I was ready. I just thought we were going to miss it and I was panicking. I'm so s–' Star stopped abruptly, looking guilty.

'Sorry?' laughed Ailsa and Star relaxed.

'I have to say, you did so well that I would never have guessed it was your first time.'

Two huge dimples appeared on her cheeks and before she rushed over to hug Ailsa, she was disturbed by another knock at the door.

'I'm popular this morning,' Ailsa said as she went to open the door, but it was pushed open before she reached it and Sylvia entered.

'Have you heard?' she said.

The two younger women looked at each other, baffled.

'Dinsmore Haigh?'

'Oh God, I haven't killed him, have I? breathed Ailsa while Star looked horrified at the possibility. Sylvia burst out laughing.

'No, she said, but... perhaps you want to sit down?'

'Tell me!' Ailsa said urgently.

'My dear, remember, 'harm to none'? Sit down.'

All three sat at the table, then Ailsa jumped up to put the kettle on before Sylvia stopped her and pointed to the chair. Ailsa sat.

'I have had a phone call from Pam, whose nephew works for the fire service.'

' Oh God,' Ailsa covered her face.

'Ailsa!'

'Okay, okay, I'm listening.'

 They were at the Haighs' farmhouse most of the night.'

 Both Ailsa and Star swallowed hard but they daren't say anything.

'Dinsmore Haigh called them there after a flash of lightning set fire to the barn full of old hay next to the farmhouse.'

'Just the barn, then,' Ailsa said with relief.

'With the barn being attached, the strong winds blew sparks onto the roof of the farmhouse, which spread to the timbers. Soon, the whole top floor of the farmhouse was on fire. They managed to put both fires out after a struggle lasting hours but the fire had reached the boiler room...'

Sylvia paused for effect.

'...damaging the pipes there, causing them to burst, flooding the downstairs area completely.'

Sylvia was smiling quite happily at this. Ailsa remembered her conversation about evil running in families, but still couldn't quite believe it of Sylvia.

'That's awful. However bad a person is, that's still a terrible thing to happen. They've been horrible to me, but they didn't deserve that.'

'I might agree with you if it weren't for the fact that the Haighs will get a massive insurance payout. According to Pam's nephew, there's the damage to the hay, the fire damage to both buildings and the flood damage, all insured and all covered. The firemen said he was actually laughing.'

Both the younger women frowned. Why was money more important to some people than anything else?

'One of them who knows quite a bit about him reckons he had insured it so high as he was going to set fire to it as a last resort if things got worse, but this has actually helped him. I knew he would come out smelling of roses but you still have your, or Effie's, revenge.

'Of course,' continued Sylvia, 'he was on the verge of bankruptcy. He was a gambler, so don't feel sorry for him. He's squandered whatever money he earned from the farm. I honestly don't think that Lulu has a clue.'

'What will he do now? Where will he go?'

'His sister in Wales is putting him up until they can find rented accommodation. I doubt he'll be back before the farmhouse is rebuilt, which will take a long time.'

'Is that what he's doing? Rebuilding it?'

'He'll be back eventually, unfortunately. It burned down in Boaz Haigh's time, remember and the Haighs still came back to infest the district when it was rebuilt. While he's away. I suggest you reinstate your ownership of Chanter's Hill so he can't get anywhere near it on his return.'

'Oh, I will, you can be assured of that.'

Now that they knew no one had been harmed and, incredibly, that Haigh might even profit out of it, both she and Star had started to relax a little until something else occurred to her.

'Was it us last night? Was it me?' she said in a croaky voice, 'did I cause it?'

Sylvia put her hands on Ailsa's shoulders.

'Fire and flood. Natural disasters aren't they? Act of God, or Gods, perhaps. The weather has been muggy for a couple of days and a storm has been threatening.'

'But one wasn't forecast,' put in Star.

'These things happen. Nature is stronger than all of us. Maybe Mother Nature heard you, though? Maybe you helped things on their way, but I don't suppose we'll ever know.'

261

Yet the look in Sylvia's eyes, the look on Star's face and the feeling in her own mind made Ailsa doubt that last statement.

'Well, aren't you going to ask?'

Sylvia's tone of voice puzzled Ailsa.

'Ask?'

'What else Pam said, or have you forgotten the meeting about your festival was this morning?' she asked incredulously.

'I've had a very strange 24 hours, and yes, it had slipped my mind. Are you going to tell us? Oh,' something occurred to Ailsa, 'wasn't Dinsmore Haigh there?'

'He was otherwise tied up,' said Sylvia, 'with all the insurers and fire officers at the farm. So, of course that meant that–'

'He couldn't scare them half to death at the meeting. He couldn't hold anything over them.'

'Correct. They had all heard about his predicament and Pam said that despite some of the more unscrupulous ones being short of a few bungs in the future, there was a collective sigh of relief around the table.

'And?' squeaked Star, unable to wait any longer.

'And, the motion has been passed to allow you to hold your festivals for the foreseeable future. It's very doubtful that it would ever be overturned after all this, although you would still have to apply on a yearly basis, but more as a formality.'

Ailsa jumped up and pulled Sylvia and Star to her in a group hug and started jumping up and down with delight, while Sylvia tutted before remembering something else.

'Starting with the next one on your list at Lammas, so you're free to start planning for that.'

'Hurray,' Star shouted, waving her hands in the air, while Ailsa collapsed on the chair. The enormity of the struggle and how it had affected her was just hitting her. Sylvia squeezed her shoulder.

Ailsa looked at these people whom she had become incredibly fond of in such a short time. She blinked the happy tears out of her eyes and stood up.

'But first, we have a party to plan!'

Chapter 27

Nightowl's Hide was a hive of industry. Preparations were being made for a Midsummer party. A party, not a festival. For friends, not for paying guests. For a smaller gathering and not a larger crowd.

Ailsa was doing something she detested in others, pacing up and down, mobile phone jammed to her ear, oblivious to the outside world. Yet, if she were to show she would not be beaten, then this small demonstration of her resolve must go ahead.

Her old band, Ashwood, had been invited. She could put three of them up in her spare bedrooms and Star said she would let the other one stay at her place.

She had been over to Farstone and invited the whole crowd en masse. She laughed to herself. These people, who had seemed like strangers at times, now seemed like family. Which, according to Peggy, most of them were.

She went round the village of Hatton-le-Hollow with small envelopes enclosing an invitation to a Midsummer's Eve party. Dinsmore and Lulu Haig, of course, were not included but they had probably gone down to Wales by now anyway.

With the help of Ade and his family - for free because they were invited and were promised ale - fairy lights went up inside the roundhouse and outside over the entrance. Others were strung across the tree branches and the stage area.

The roundhouse had acquired a name, displayed proudly on a wooden board above the entrance - Lilith's Barn - with a carving of a barn owl next to the lettering.

The stage, put up as a temporary measure, was placed further down the land, facing up towards Lilith Barn, with a hastily constructed half-moon roof covering the rear, so hopefully it would prevent any noise reaching the residents who didn't attend. She intended to go around and ask those people if the sound had disturbed them afterwards. Yes, she was covering all bases but she genuinely didn't want to fall out with this village. Her village.

Food was arranged through Esme's bakery, not selling though, as Ailsa had covered the cost herself. After all, it was a private party.

This was her world and had been for 15 years. People gathering together, enjoying themselves, all accompanied by the folk traditions of long ago, which were thankfully being continued.

There had always been a strong belief in folklore all around these Yorkshire moorland villages, including the songs, dances and storytelling of the area. She intended to showcase local and traditional crafts for the proper festivals.

She was bringing these folk traditions back to the village of Hatton-le-Hollow and was doing her favourite thing in the world. Singing. When she sang these old songs and even the newer ones in the same vein, she felt alive. Energised. She felt the nearest thing to happiness she had ever experienced.

Vinny, one of the band, was a barbecue fanatic and she had availed herself readily of his offer to provide one for the night.

The wash house was now imaginatively named The Washhouse on the plaque above the door from the local craftsman who made the Lilith's Barn sign. It was to all intents and purposes, up and running. It just needed a few finishing touches but they could wait.

She had phoned to ask Elspeth and Tess from Weaver's Green to the party. They had regretfully declined, as they always did Midsummer's Eve celebration at their own village but promised to attend the next gathering.

Sylvia said she had invited Pam and her family and she'd happily accepted. Ailsa was glad of this. Not because she was a council member against Haigh, but because she genuinely liked the woman.

Conall asked if it was all right for him and his fellow players to perform there and to turn into strolling players when people were eating and Ailsa accepted like a shot. She was dying to hear what they sounded like as she had heard nothing but praise from Stan and Star.

She didn't know how she felt about the Storyteller's inclusion at the party. Whether he'd been invited by those at Farstone or whether he'd invited himself, she wasn't sure- but he was going to be there. She was worried the younger ones would be scared of him; she felt a bit that way herself, but according to Sylvia, everyone just accepted him. He was, after all, part of the folklore around these parts himself.

Ailsa concluded that he must somehow appear different to different people at the same time. She didn't want to think about it too much, her brain was already near to exploding with all the Midsummer party preparations.

Inside Lilith's Barn, trestle tables were set up and she had ordered long solid wood benches for either side of all the tables. She wanted it to be a communal experience rather than everyone at their own small tables, not sharing or joining in the conversation. She had in mind something like the old Viking mead halls, where they would feast on food and drink and tell stories and old songs, which sometimes ended up with fights to prove their alpha supremacy. She couldn't see that happening here now that Dinsmore Haigh had left, although she wasn't quite sure about Ade and his family after a few glasses of mead.

Lots of 'seconds' from a pottery nearby had given her plates, bowls and mugs. Even as seconds, they were a little expensive, but they were an investment for future festivals. If there were any further festivals. Ailsa stopped that train of thought and looked at her list. She ticked off glasses. Not glass, but recycled plastic and biodegradable within 12 months.

She hadn't asked the villagers to RSVP. There wasn't any time, but just asked them to turn up on the Saturday. She wanted it to be relaxed, not formal. In a way, it was a dry run for the festivals, as she wanted the same thing from them.

A large fire pit was placed outside in a special stone-built circle. There was the one inside the barn too, where the boys had made a central stone fireplace. This would have to burn smokeless fire logs to comply with fire regulations. It would still have the same effect, so Ailsa wasn't worried.

Doubtless, many more things she should have done would occur to her at the last minute, but for now, all that was to be done was to go to bed early. She had to be up at a silly hour to continue with her preparations, getting everything set out. It was going to be hard work, but she found she was really looking forward to it. Small gatherings were what she enjoyed. The sort where you could have a word with everyone there and people went home happy.

There was a knock at the door just then, Stan from The Falcon.

'Where do you want these?' he grinned. She directed him to the barn. Behind him, on a sort of handcart, were boxes of ale. Lots of them. Behind that was Dan, one of the barmen, with another handcart containing large bottles of cider, individual bottles of cider and bottles of red and white wine. No one who drank spirits was catered for – it was take it or leave it- but this little lot should keep everyone happy, maybe *too* happy.

Stan was letting Ailsa have it all at cost. He didn't lose anything, but he didn't make anything either, bless him. The only other drink was the mead, which she always bought from the same suppliers. The ones who had supplied some of the festivals over the years. Mead was the only drink she truly liked the taste of, but because it was so sweet and easy to drink, people sometimes didn't realise it could blow your head off. She had already prepared little notices, MEAD DRINKER, BEWARE. The Merry Mead company were delivering in the morning and staying for the party. They were bringing a tent, being hardened campers.

Just as she climbed into her bed, she had an awful thought. All that alcohol in the barn wasn't behind locked doors. No one in the village would take it and no one else knew where it was, but.... Dinsmore Haigh popped into her mind and wouldn't pop back out. What if he was still hanging around? What if he hadn't gone to Wales yet?

Maybe she should go up there to sleep, to protect the place? Maybe Lilith would protect it? Almost as soon as the thought formed in her mind, a ghost cry came from further down the land. A night owl's screech. She smiled to herself. There was no need to worry; Lilith was already there, protecting her barn.

Chapter 28

Merry Mead were delivering the bottles before she got into compos mentis mode. Still in her pyjamas, she answered the door to an eye roll from Biba, the owner and long-time friend of Ailsa's.

'Having a lie in again, are we?' She gave her throaty laugh. It was 6:05 a.m. so Ailsa gave her a 'look'.

'When are the boys arriving?' Biba continued.

The 'boys' were Ailsa's old band, Ashwood, and definitely not boys anymore.

'They'll be here at a decent hour, I expect, unlike some. If you weren't carrying mead, I might not have let you in.'

They grinned and hugged, then she directed her and the others - her partner and her two brothers - up to the barn.

She made a large pot of coffee, put that and mugs, milk and sugar on the kitchen table, then left the door unlocked for them. She showered and changed into jeans and a t-shirt, which said on the front. 'It'll be reet, so...' and on the back '...sit thissen dahn an' ah'll put t'kettle on'.

She'd never really had this accent, although this was more West/South Yorkshire rather than North, but she found herself wishing that she had a Yorkshire inflection.. She was proud now to be born and raised in Yorkshire, even if the rest of her life was a blur of Southern counties and cities. She frowned, then gave a chuckle. Her thinking had changed so much in a few months that she hardly recognised herself.

Esme and her assistant came early to set up a stall, but she was bringing the food later, just before it started. The gates were opening at 3:00 p.m. It was, after all, a Midsummer's Eve party and she hoped that some would stay to see the sunrise the next morning as well as the sunset tonight. They may have missed the solstice, but Midsummer's Eve, when the veil between the two worlds was at its thinnest and witches and fairies could be seen, was just as important.

Those with children, such as Jennet and Steve Cayley with the twins and many of the villagers, would go home well before this. Of course, that was if any of them turned up in the first place. It was short notice for everyone, she knew, and even though they might not object to her gatherings, taking part in them might be a different thing.

Stan had set up a bar on the trestle table in the barn. As he reckoned most people would be celebrating here, he and Dan, the barman would be running it from 4:00 p.m. onwards while Dan went back at 7:00 p.m. in case there was anything doing - but with the proviso that if the pub was dead, he could put up a sign outside saying 'Pub Closed. Go next door for a party!'.

3:00 p.m. arrived. The day had been hot and setting it up had seemed like hard work, with sweat pouring off them. The temperature hadn't dropped and the heat was still beating down. It gave everything a lazy feel about it, like everyone should relax instead of rushing around. There was a heat haze shimmering, reminding them that the sun was at its full power.

In the village, the Green was green, the sky was blue and Hatton Beck sparkled in the sunshine- a white wooden bridge spanning its banks. The stone cottages all around were a mellow ochre colour and everything was quiet and sleepy.

Out of those stone cottages came the occupants, of all ages and they were dressed according to the weather, but with rucksacks on their backs with waterproof coats hanging over them. This *was* England, after all. They also carried blankets and folding chairs. These were people set on enjoying themselves as they all made their way to Nightowl's Hide.

An hour earlier, the boys of Ashwood had arrived in a large van. This one was an improvement on the one they had started out with, when they were lucky to reach their destination without leaving various bits of the van on the roads leading to it.

The Farstone contingent arrived just after 3:00 p.m., having taken the wise decision to hire a bus which just about squeezed them all in. The driver, Anthony, was a resident of their village and a strict teetotaller, which came in handy normally, although he was camping in the bus tonight to take them back in the morning.

Surprisingly, most of the Farstone contingent had brought tents. The younger ones, anyway. Peggy and Binky, she knew, were staying at Sylvia's. Flora and Cal were staying in her bedroom as he refused to let his pregnant partner camp out, even though Flora was all for the idea. Philippa, Jerry and Mary had shut up the Peverel Inn for the day. They all hugged her tightly and Philippa whispered. 'Welcome back, my love, home at last', which touched her deeply.

274

Cal and Conall were chatting in a friendly way, but with no indication that they were anything more than acquaintances, despite the affirmation that they were distantly related, then she remembered her connection with Effie Bothwell. You could fry your brain trying to work it all out. They did look alike, though....

Pam had turned up with her family and joined in with the Farstone villagers, whom she obviously knew. She hugged Ailsa and offered her support in the future and was assured she would avail herself of that offer if Dinsdale Haigh showed his face.

All the campers, she knew, would be hoping to make it through the night without sleep, just so they could see the sunrise on what marked the middle of summer and the arrival of days of warmth, light and abundance. Ailsa intended to camp out too. Been there, done that and would happily do it again.

At the moment, Conall's players were indeed strolling through the arrivals, playing the flute, the lute and the bodhran. Ailsa had been told they were being very well received, but sadly, hadn't had time to listen properly.

She was amazed at the number of villagers who had turned up, some even getting into the spirit of things by wearing flowers or herbs around their necks or in their hair. She hadn't got a photographic memory, but it seemed like the whole village had come here to enjoy themselves, although it *was* only a small village.

For the first time, Ailsa felt that it wasn't just that they wanted to support her, which would have been enough anyway, but they really wanted to come here to have a good time. Somewhere they could walk to and have a few drinks with no transport worries, and then walk back whenever they felt like it. She was meeting and greeting as many people as she could. She owed it to them all. This was the moment she felt they had accepted her - and that she had accepted this village as her home. She decided there and then that there would always be a free gathering for the locals, once a year, in recognition of their support. A huge Hatton-le-Hollow party. Entertainment would be free as would tea, coffee and water – but the stalls would be able to charge for their produce – and Stan could run the bar as otherwise he would be losing out at the pub.

She turned around, prompted by a tap on the shoulder, to see Star holding out a small wreath of flowers, similar to the one she herself wore. She stretched up to press it down onto Ailsa's head.

She then bent down to retrieve a package leaning against her legs and handed it to Ailsa with a shy smile. Ailsa opened it to reveal neatly folded bunting. Star gave one end to Sylvia, who stood nearby and walked away so that they could see it all.

The long banner had triangular, coloured cotton pennants - beautifully sewn - and each with a motif on one side. The sun was represented many times in different styles, as was the moon, both full and crescent. Flowers, herbs and stags, then, dotted throughout, was Lilith, the white barn owl. Ailsa looked closer. Her own name was there in the middle, embroidered under the rebuilt version of Nightowl's Hide and on either side were representations of Lilith's Barn.

Ailsa stared at it for ages, immobile. She slowly turned towards Star, whose happy smile had started to disappear, confused by the silence.

Suddenly, and she didn't know exactly how it happened, she was standing there next to the unfurled bunting and sobbing her heart out. Real tears coursing down her cheeks. She couldn't understand it. She had never been one to cry easily. She wasn't cold as much as non-empathetic, but that seemed to have changed in a big way. Clinging onto the other end of the bunting, a still-confused-looking Star walked tentatively towards her.

'Are you alright?' she whispered hesitantly.

She got her answer as Ailsa flung herself at Star, hugging her so tightly that Sylvia didn't know whether Star's red face was flushing with pleasure or because she was having the breath crushed out of her. Possibly just in time, Ailsa released her.

'I really, *really*, don't know how to thank you. It's perfect. I'm going to have it in Lilith's Barn. Unless you would like it somewhere else?'

'No! There, is where I imagined it to be. I made it especially for you.' Star's face was beaming again.

'I know, and I think that's what got to me. All the work, all the hours, all the care that's gone into that. It's so special. Thank you, Star,' and she hugged her again, this time without imitating a boa constrictor.

When she looked up, tears were rolling down Star's cheeks too. Ailsa's lips quivered and, not wanting to let herself down a second time, she sniffed, drew a hand across her cheeks and said,

'I'll have to go inside to repair my make-up now. Look what you've done to me.'

Star laughed and Ailsa managed a tremulous smile before quickly escaping to Nightowl's Hide.

Sylvia took in her reaction as did Peggy and Binky, and they all exchanged knowing glances. Sylvia turned and watched Ailsa walk away.

'Welcome home,' she whispered.

278

Ashwood had just played an acoustic set on the stage to enthusiastic applause from the audience. Ailsa couldn't stop the wide grin on her face. Cain waved to her and she waved back happily. This is what she thought it would be like. Her dream was coming true.

As she watched, the audience started to drift off up to Lilith's Barn. Ailsa was puzzled. Had there been an announcement she had missed? She thought she knew the itinerary. Maybe they were going to eat in there, but none of them had stopped at Esme's stall. Besides, most people had been lounging about on the grass, eating her food, well before now. She followed them, intrigued.

Then suddenly, there he was, the Storyteller or Culhain, standing in front of where her altar was. She concentrated on him, watching him intently, but every time she thought she was about to see his face, her thoughts distracted her and she was back to square one. She gave up and instead watched his slim, ageless figure in ragged, dirty green and brown clothes, as though he'd been sleeping rough, with his hood pulled far down over his face. He moved like a cat, a silent tiger.

When he started to speak, the background murmuring stopped and became a complete silence. Ailsa noticed this as though in a dream, as she too seemed to be caught in his spell. His voice, quiet, yet reaching to each one of them, began-

THE STORYTELLER'S TALE.

Good day to you all. Let me introduce myself. I am the Storyteller – perhaps you've heard of me? No matter - but tell me, do you believe in the supernatural?

Perhaps I can persuade you? Shall we see? Listen closely and let me tell you of the other world, the magical world, the surreal world you would like to believe in, but can't quite bring yourself to do so. The world that exists all around you, one of many such worlds that are on different planes of existence.

*I see your faces and recognise the expressions of disbelief. The absolute knowledge that the world **you** know is the only possible one.*

All of you gathered here have heard the old stories. The stories of Midsummer. How we burned fires, danced and sang, honouring the sun, knowing that it was at the peak of its power and would make these lands fertile so we could all live.

281

*These rites are almost as old as the Earth itself and they still happen today - as they are happening right here at this moment. Do you know why? Because most people still believe. All of you here believe, or you wouldn't be here today. Yes, you will enjoy the music. Yes, you will enjoy the food, the fire, the dance, the reasons you **thought** you were here. Yet through an inherent feeling, you will enjoy being part of something that you can connect to, that is inborn in all of you. At the back of your minds, you believe in the old and the new world being as one. The old traditions continue almost seamlessly throughout the centuries, living in the subconscious of all of you.*

This land was once steeped in folklore and superstition, many, many years ago. People lived their lives by it and for it. They were closer to Nature than you are now. They existed alongside Nature because they lived off the land. It led their existence.

They knew that on Midsummer's Eve, when the veil between the Earth and the Faery realm was at its thinnest, the Fae crossed over to join us for a while. To walk the land, to communicate with the Druids, to talk with the witches.

Yet it wasn't the only time. Throughout each year, they used portals to cross from the Faery realm. Stone gateways from another dimension where the Fae exist in a less substantial form than on this Earth, being mostly composed of the wind and the air around them and of the light prisms that shine down from their sky. Their form is like yours, yet not as solid.

You may have heard of one of these portals? The Faestone. Up on the moors and where Farstone gets its name. A portal which shifts position so no human can ever find it and enter, so losing their Earthbound home. Condemned to wander the Faerie lands forever.

Here, the Fae usually lived among the trees and woodland, which covered much of the land, the oxygen produced by the trees being beneficial to them. In your world, they had corporeal form and looked very like you. There were differences, as the Fae could still use their magic. Physically, they had a unique grace of movement and a pleasing form. Whether or not people feared or revered them, they at least believed in them.

As time went on, the old ways began to disappear and people stopped believing. These old traditions were frowned on in the name of the new Christianity sweeping the land. This new religion reared its head in the name of one God and went against the nature of the land.

The Church replaced what they thought were evil Pagan ways with something much worse- the oppression of the people and the suppression of free will. Pagans didn't cause wars, yet this new religion did. Countless people fought and died in the name of this new God.

Many witches too, were put to death for knowing the ways of the land and for healing people. Natural ways. They were blamed for the lies spread about them, of which there were many.

You know of one who lived here on this land you stand on now. She suffered for the ignorance of her fellow men - and you honour her today, whether you know it or not.

Druids, the wise ones, all but disappeared from our lands, only recently reappearing and, once again, working with Nature and the elements.

And the Fae, the least known of all of them. The Fae. Faeries. Does anyone believe in Faeries anymore? No? Perhaps that should change?

You believe in witches and Druids because, in the main, you know they belong to the race of humans. Yet, what if there was another race that lived on this land and in other lands, living alongside you but mostly unrecognised by the human race? Can anyone really think that there are nothing but humans living here, and not accept the possibility of beings from another plane, another dimension, existing amongst them?

284

Long ago, the Fae were known and accepted by people who were themselves once believed to be supernatural, the witches and the Druids.

There were many witches living around these parts. You've all heard of the Witches of Farstone, along the edge of Farstone Moor, who had lived there since the village began. Perhaps they are still there?

As Christianity has begun a gradual decline, the old traditions are coming to the fore again and are becoming stronger as the world turns back to Nature. Witches are tolerated, as are the new Druids - but this may be too late for the Fae.

The pure Fae can no longer exist in your world. Their bodies, once almost solid here, are fading away. It is not only the escalation of chemicals and pollutants into the air which shortens their lives. They have been all but banished from these lands for many years. They fear for the existence of their race in the world which has emerged here. They fear for yours, too. And, they cannot live in a world where they are not accepted and where they are condemned to the world of storybooks.

What should the Fae do to avoid having to leave these lands altogether? Is it possible for you to accept the existence of these Faery Folk? What can be done to let the Fae live peacefully amongst

285

you? The portals between this world and that of the Fae will soon close altogether, unless acceptance of this generally peaceful race of beings is achieved.

Yet, the world is not a peaceful place and is becoming less tolerant every day. You all know this. Poison is running riot in this world. Not only in the air but between men. There is anger, bitterness, and persecution. Vile outpourings of hatred amongst you. The acceptance of another race, a peaceful race, not of this world, is unthinkable.

There has been a long history of the two races living alongside each other on this earth. Did you not know? Perhaps you people here are thinking of fairies with gossamer wings and elfin faces, possibly only as small as a mistle thrush or less?

Yet, what if they strode amongst you unknown and unrecognised? What if they looked like you and your neighbours? What if they have married humans or bred with them to produce offspring - halflings- in order to perpetuate their race? There has always been a great attraction between Fae and humans, on both sides. Halflings are far stronger in this world than pure-bred Fae.

Would this be fair, do you think? In order to continue their existence on this earth, could this be the only way? By diluting their blood with yours

286

but still preserving the age-old ancestry? To be part of an Ancient Alliance between humans and Fae from the beginning of time, but one that has been long forgotten. Do the Fae, at this moment, walk amongst you, unnoticed, apart from the few who know them to be different or 'other?.

Do they even need your acceptance? Is it just because they want it, rather than need it? Would you ever even know if the whole population of the Fae realm, strengthened by the ties with humans, came to live amongst you? You might feel that there is something a little strange about them. Something you can't quite put your finger on, but would you really ever know for sure?

Perhaps your neighbour has Fae blood? Perhaps some of your family carries Fae blood from way back. One of the half-blood Fae could be the person you have fallen in love with, the one who has tended your lands, healed your animals, and healed humans, too. They could be the ones who have helped the poor, shielded the abused and helped to stop wars. How would you know?

You must accept the possibility, otherwise, the whole history of the Fae on this Earth will be forgotten. Wiped out by ignorance and a belief that humans are the only ones that exist in this whole universe.

The story I have told you today may be the truth, of course, but as my profession is Storyteller, it may just be a tale to make you reach beyond the limits of your imagination. To accept people who are different to you- and to continue the age-old traditions, the ancestry, the uniqueness that make this land so special, because it is your history too.

The next time that you sneer when you hear about witches, that you raise your eyes when you hear about Druids and when you laugh at people who believe in the Fae- think again.

Open your minds and your hearts. Accept that your race, the human race, though important to all of you dwelling here, is nothing compared to the enormity, the magic and the majesty of Nature. You must all return to Nature eventually to save your souls.

Accept that everyone and everything on this Earth is part of that Nature and, whether you know it or not, there is a reason that you are all here.

Chapter 29

Walking slowly away from the barn, Ailsa turned to Peggy in a daze, shaking her head.

'I just listened intently to his story- but I can't remember much about it. Can you?'

'Yes, I can,' replied. Peggy, before demonstrating her twitch of a smile.

'Ask me,' said Sylvia.

'Can you remember?' asked Ailsa, dutifully.

'Only that it was about the Fae.' Sylvia replied with a vacant smile.

'I had a vague idea it wasn't suitable for the children who were listening? Don't know why though!' Ailsa laughed.

'Yet,' interrupted Peggy, you will remember his words, as will the other listeners. It is told this way so the children *don't* worry, but will still be impressed. The words will be ingrained in their subconscious, as they will in yours. You will never

289

forget them, even if you don't know why they are there. If you were wholly aware, you might have been slightly alarmed if you were impressionable. This is his talent, his gift as a storyteller.'

Peggy kept to herself, as she always did, that it was a form of hypnotism, a form of 'glamour' used by the Fae. She knew the ones whose blood had been diluted could not use this 'glamour', not on purpose anyway, as they didn't know they possessed it. Yet Culhain was a messenger who moved between the Fae and the human world and had far less of the human characteristics than the earthbound ones of Fae ancestry did. She occasionally communicated with him but couldn't let anyone know. It was a responsibility which weighed heavily on her, as she was uneasy around him. He had a power that, after all these years, she didn't understand.

'You heard it all, so are you alarmed?' asked Sylvia, already knowing the answer. 'No, because I'm not impressionable.'

Ailsa started to wonder what the point of a storyteller was if people didn't remember his story, but two minutes later, she couldn't even bring to mind what *Peggy* had told her, let alone the Storyteller.

*

290

The people all moved on to the food, with plates in hand and a sudden hunger in their stomachs. There were chicken slices, cheese and onion slices, steak pies and veg pies, all with the wonderful light touch with pastry that Esme produced. There were rice salads, pasta salads and normal salads. There were herby new potatoes, potato salad and coleslaw. There were - crusty on the outside and soft inside - bread cakes, Esme's speciality, with either white or wholemeal flour.

There was smoke coming from a table set up further down the land, along with an enticing smell which drifted over the mostly recumbent figures. Burgers and sausages, normal and veggie, were being dished out, accompanied by Esme's bread cakes and rolls.

Stan was doing a roaring trade in alcohol and soft drinks. He had moved a smaller table outside, and Dan was dishing out freshly made, real lemonade from there with a constant supply of ice cubes brought up from Ailsa's freezer.

Most people were taking advantage of the beautiful weather and eating in the fresh air, but some preferred a bit of shade and were sitting around the tables inside the barn, along with those making regular use of the bar inside.

Most people sat around on the grass, where speedwell and buttercups, daisies, wood violets and selfheal grew amongst the grass. It was growing again after it had been cut last week. Around the edges of the land, where the grass had been left to grow longer, there was wild yarrow, cow parsley and willow herb.

While they all fed themselves and relaxed, Hyrne, Conall's band, took the stage. Conall, for obvious reasons, commanded most of Ailsa's attention, but as she tore her eyes away, she found that others in the audience were mesmerised too.

Where were the other members of the band from? Not from around here, surely, as she would have seen them? They were all incredibly good-looking and would steal any young maiden's heart in the audience. Yet Conall outshone them all, or perhaps she was biased. She watched his measured, graceful movements as he made his way across the stage, striding and turning, both laid back yet with a lithe energy.

The instruments all seemed to be from a bygone day, especially the huge old wooden instrument that Conall played. He'd said it was a Shawm, a medieval instrument and the forerunner of the oboe. The music itself was old Folk, but mostly none that she had heard before, but strangely, seemed to recognise. There were hints of traditional folk, but it had more than a touch of medieval about it. However, you could describe it, the set was keeping the audience mesmerised, much as with the storyteller earlier.

When they had finished and the audience rose as one in rapturous applause, she heard a voice in her ear. Cain, her old bandmate.

'I think you found your new band,' he said quietly as he squeezed her shoulder.

She would miss Cain, she would miss all of her band, but she knew they needed peace now. They had been at this for far longer than she had. Old musicians never really retire. They just slow down and eventually fade away into the sunset. She gave him a hug and told him she would always need him, if only as a friend, but she envisaged playing many more sets with him here.

There was plenty of time till she joined Ashwood on stage for the last set of the day at 8:00 p.m. Many of the children were staying until the end of the performance, prompted perhaps by parents and grandparents who knew and liked Ailsa McKendry and Ashwood from previous performances.

The heat shimmered over the land at Nightowl's Hide, as bees buzzed around the clover patches and dragonflies skimmed above people's heads. Sparrows, bluetits, robins, finches and thrushes hadn't been worried by the music at all. In fact, Ailsa noted that later, as dusk fell, they seemed to join in, singing happily from their perches in the hedges and trees on the perimeter.

There was a lazy feel to everything. Everyone was so relaxed and laid back. Local villagers were speaking to Farstone villagers as though they were old friends and the bands integrated with their audience when not performing on stage and were warmly welcomed.

Ailsa closed her eyes, processing it all in her thoughts. She sighed with pleasure. She couldn't have imagined it going any better and took this as a very good omen for the proper festivals.

A chord, played on the stage, made her open her eyes wide. She couldn't believe the completely unscheduled event taking place in front of her now. Members of both Ashwood and Hyrne had joined together in an unholy alliance and were producing a lively set, with the aim of getting everyone on their feet.

People were dancing round energetically in circles, linking arms, then carrying on to the next person in the circle. Others were doing their own form of a jig and the children were whirling round and laughing uproariously. Dogs were running round having the time of their lives and Ailsa had to laugh at Wolf and Coco, jumping around together as though they were dancing. One jumping back while the other put their head on their paws mischievously and then swapping their 'dance movements' around. They seemed to be the most unlikely 'best of pals'. There were only four songs, but it was probably just enough in this heat.

Ailsa accidentally lay on the Witch-stone she carried with her today for Midsummer's Eve, so she decided to test it out to see if she could see any fairies or witches. She smiled dismissively to herself as she held it up to her eye, but she was in the mood to try anything. You could see fairies or witches through the hole in the stone on Midsummer's Eve, according to tradition, but she could hardly see a thing through it. Maybe the hole was too small.

She managed at last to focus clearly on Conall on the stage, but she had hardly taken her eyes off him since he went up there, so that wasn't a surprise. Then, after another couple of minutes of trying while scanning the audience, she found herself looking at Peggy. Well, that was right, as, in all probability, she *was* a witch.

Annoyingly, she couldn't focus on anyone else. Apart from a figure on the edge of Chanter's Hill, who looked very much like Culhain, the Storyteller. What was he doing there?

She frowned. Only three people? Why wouldn't it let her look at any of the audience? There was a cold feeling in the pit of her stomach as she held the stone up to see Conall again. Instead, she found herself looking at the figure on Chanter's Hill. After a second or two, she couldn't remember what she was doing with the stone in her hand or why she had started this. She laughed at herself, returning the stone to her pocket and joined in with the songs again.

On the last song, Conall deserted his post and, jumping off the stage, made straight for her.

'Oh no,' she said, making defensive arm movements, but he ignored them. He grasped her hand- again, that electric shock through her body at his touch - and pulled her up. Soon, she was whirling round under his arm, laughing as she held both his hands and twirled around at a dizzying speed. At the end, she collapsed into his arms, as happy and giddy as any of the laughing children.

Eventually, everyone sat down on the grass once again, ready for a rest, and the cold drinks did a roaring trade. Dusk fell, the birds sang and the murmur of gentle conversation was heard.

At last, it was time for Ailsa's own performance and an uncharacteristic flutter of butterflies in her stomach surprised her. She never experienced nerves. She knew her songs and her audience inside out. Was it perhaps that this time it mattered to her more? It was in front of her friends, her family, and the local villagers who had made her more than welcome. She didn't want to let any of them down. As she climbed onto the stage, there was a huge round of spontaneous applause, which encouraged her, making the butterflies fly away.

There was a silence, then her strong, sure, natural-born gift of a voice soared above them and among them, enveloping them all and commanding their attention. The band joined in after the first verse. She had hooked them, those who didn't already know of her talent.

Soon, the soaring vocals were accompanied by cheering, clapping, and whoops of delight with the magical results of all the audience joining in the choruses, encouraged by Cain, who Ailsa had never seen as animated.

They did three encores, the last of which had everyone on their feet, dancing and cheering, bringing them firmly past their original cut-off time of 10:00 p.m.

They reluctantly finished, and Ailsa made a speech thanking everyone - locals, friends and family - who had helped. She told them, as a token of her appreciation, that there would be a party here once a year for them all, entry and entertainment free of charge.

Then, surprisingly, Sylvia took the stage and, turning the tables, thanked Ailsa for bringing the whole community together.

Everyone clapped and cheered so loudly that Ailsa found herself thinking that it was a good job the Haighs *had* left the village, or there would most definitely be a barrage of complaints from them.

Chapter 30

The evening brought a bucolic stillness and a lethargy over the remaining people there. The only ones to leave were those with children, who had already stayed up well beyond their bedtime and had thoroughly enjoyed it. They would sleep well tonight with all the fresh air and excitement.

Some of the locals had even brought tents so they could stay with the older children to watch the sunrise, which promised to be an excellent one.

People were still in their vests, t-shirts and shorts, or flowery thin dresses, with coats abandoned next to their rucksacks. Amazingly, many were still eating as the witching hour approached, although they were mostly eating cheese and biscuits, which were all that was left. Drinks had just about dried up, but Stan, bless him, had nipped next door for top-ups. In general, people had slowed down and whereas some slept until others woke them up, most managed to stay awake until the early sunrise of Midsummer's Day. Disappointingly, Conall seemed to have disappeared, along with the rest of Hyrne, around midnight. Therefore, Ailsa was ridiculously pleased to see him turn up a while later, just as she was thinking of going to sit in her tent, cross-legged at the open entrance, like a guru, waiting for the dawn by herself.

Conall made for her as though he were fitted with radar. The fairy lights made more of an ambient lighting and enabled people to see the shapes of others rather than identify faces from a distance. He sat next to her on the blankets. Wolf, by his side as usual, lay down beside them with his head on his big paws and went to sleep.

There was an air of expectation hanging in the air all around them. Ailsa reached down onto the grass in front of them and lit a candle, which jumped and flickered over their faces. Conall pulled an incense holder and joss sticks from his inside pockets, which he lit on the ground near to the candle. Smoke whirled and eddied, wafting towards them, with an unrecognisable fragrance which tantalised the senses.

She closed her eyes and smiled. She was happy. She couldn't remember feeling this happy since, well...ever. She could feel the warmth of

Conall's skin next to hers as he lay back. They both looked up to the sky. To the moon, to the stars, to the universe- and they both felt part of it. Part of a greater Natural creation.

Ailsa propped herself up and looked around her. She could see people waiting expectantly. What did the midsummer sunrise mean for them? New Hope? New beginnings? Because this is what it meant to her. She could make out the Farstone contingent, still all there, including Jennet's twins, who were fast asleep on the blanket. She could make out Flora, who blew a kiss across to her, as though she knew what she was thinking. She blew one back.

Sylvia was there- she raised her hand in greeting to Ailsa, who did the same in return. Star was there next to Sylvia, Amos and Esme. She could make out the tubby mound of Charm, asleep on her legs. These people, all these people, had suddenly become very important to her. If, indeed, they were all related from somewhere back in time, she was very happy for it to be so.

Night creatures on wings wafted across in front of the fairy lights - and the lanterns and candles which people had placed next to them on the ground. There was an ambience of calm and content amongst them as well as a feeling of anticipation.

Time passed as Ailsa and Conall talked in a low whisper to each other. They talked about today and what it meant for the future. They talked about the future and what it meant for them. They talked of animals, birds, nature, music, history, and the moors around them. The History of the Farstone moors, its ancient history and how it affected them. Then they lay back in silence for a while, holding hands and staring upwards.

After a while, the sky, previously a light to mid purple colour, as it had never reached true black, started to alter. There was a murmur of expectation across the people around her. As they all watched, the sky changed, almost without them noticing. There was a light-coloured mistiness around them. Everyone sat up, eager not to miss a second.

The sun started to appear above the horizon, red, orange, gold - almost as though it had been placed there by magic.

Conall nudged Ailsa and pointed across to Chanter's Hill, where there was a silhouette of a large bird, perched in the branches of the trees there, its head turned towards the emerging sun. Conall saluted Lilith and Ailsa followed suit.

The sun's brilliance merged into the purple sky above, a single purple line reaching across the golden orb. Gradually, the sun rose, its edges undefined, melting into an emerging Midsummer's Day sky.

She looked at Conall, who smiled and reached down to place the gentlest and sweetest of kisses on her lips. Suddenly, he pulled back and Ailsa followed his eye line. A large white bird swooped down over their heads and went to rest further down on the wall of Ailsa's new garden, as if to announce her intention to guard the land and the cottage.

As the early dawn replaced the mellow orange/yellow light of sunrise with a brighter, starker light, albeit still with a blue mist nearer to the ground, people began making for their tents or their homes in the village, or their beds for the night.

Conall put his arm around Ailsa and they made their way towards Nightowl's Hide, where her friends and relatives stayed. They paused for a moment and then carried on, hand in hand, with Wolf leading the way, across the moors to the Shepherd's Hut, waiting for them in the new dawn.

As they climbed the steps, out of the corner of her eye, she saw a white, undefined shape standing at the edge of the trees. Then Conall smiled at her and she took his hand.

The sun rose in the sky, bathing the tips of the purple heather and showing its brilliance. As he pulled her inside, she looked in the direction of the village, hidden in a green-leafed dip in the moors - and more than any other time of her life, she knew true happiness and a wonderful sense of belonging.

Epilogue

The gates to Nightowl's Cottage were thrown open for the first official festival since Ailsa had moved to Hatton-le-Hollow. People from all over poured into the grounds, but many she recognised from earlier small festivals she had played at.

The place was soon full of people, yet it was still an intimate gathering, which was just how she had envisioned it. Tickets had been limited, on a first-come, first-served basis, but she made sure all the important people in her life were there. This included the people of her village.

The occasion was Lughnasadh, the harvest festival dedicated to Lugh, the god of the harvest. It was held over the weekend beginning July 31st and the camping site was reassuringly full. This differed from her Midsummer party in that, as well as people paying for tickets, food, and any purchases from the craft stores, there were Morris dancers from Yorkshire performing. These included the White Rose Morris dancers, the Flamborough sword dancers and the Makara Morris, who dressed in green rags and shouted fiercely as they danced.

Lughnasadh was celebrated as a time of abundance and thanks for the harvest that had been produced from the land. It celebrated the first fruits of the harvest and the connection between all living things. It was the last celebration of Summer before Autumn appeared to mark the shortening of the days.

Representations of the god Lugh were sold, in the form of a corn circle encasing a five-pointed star, with ears of corn at each point of the star.

Again, along with the music and dancing and with the addition of the Mummers, came the Storyteller. Storytelling was an important part of the folklore of the North Yorkshire Moors. It seemed to Ailsa that he was widely accepted here, but she wasn't sure she could ever feel relaxed in his presence.

When he had told his story, which kept the audience rapt - although she, and she was sure, the audience too, couldn't remember half of what he had said - she vaguely recalled a tale about the harvest, the sun, abundance and fertility.

Afterwards, he had shocked her by bowing to her as he passed her. An old-fashioned, courteous bow, with one arm sweeping to the side. She nodded a hasty acknowledgement before he disappeared out of sight.

She walked up the land calling in at Lilith's Barn, knowing that Lilith was up Chanter's Hill, watching. People recognised Ailsa as she walked around and the locals now accepted her, not as Ailsa McKendry, the singer, but as Ailsa Reed, their neighbour.

The bands, including herself and Ashwood and Conall's Hyrne, and a few others, were a resounding success.

Dinsmore Haigh and his wife Lulu still hadn't returned to the village, so were unlikely to be disturbed by any noise.

They were on course to receive the insurance payout for a brand new farmhouse and barn. There had been a delay, but even though there were suspicions that there might have been something 'funny' going on, nothing could be proved. And, even though she would have liked to have blamed Haigh for the fire, she had a sneaking suspicion that it was more her fault than Haigh's.

Ludmilla the vampire had found out about his gambling. Word was that Lulu had said she would leave him if he didn't stop all gambling and frittering their money away. He had promised and begged her to stay, which she did, prompted, it was surmised, by the new farmhouse with all mod cons that awaited her. Was this what Conall had meant in the Shepherd's Hut that day? 'In defeating him, you will help him more than you know'.

The stalls were doing a roaring trade, especially Esme's bakery, which had been producing loaves in the shape of sheaves of corn. The other name for Lughnasadh was Lammas, which came from the old English 'hlaf-masse', meaning loaf mass. The loaves were originally offered up as a harvest thanksgiving.

Corn dollies in varying forms were being sold on stalls, as well as wooden carvings and jewellery. Jennet had set up her stall selling crystals there. As the evening wore on, fires were lit for protection and to ward off evil influences - and also to honour Lugh.

The Farstone contingent attended en masse, including Peggy, who stayed at Sylvia's. Flora and Cal had sent their apologies. Ailsa was extremely pleased to hear that Flora had just given birth to a daughter, Matilda. There was a special message to Ailsa, through Mary. She opened the envelope and read.

' I *do* have a beautiful, healthy baby girl, Ailsa. Thank you for putting my mind at rest all those months ago. Would you help Cal and me in presenting our child to the gods and goddesses of

Nature, to receive their blessings and protection? One of the godmothers, if you like.'

Ailsa was thrilled and readily accepted, relaying this message back to her through Mary.

Sylvia and Amos were there, the former giving her an affectionate kiss on her cheek. She told Ailsa she was proud of her, which meant so much to her. Sylvia had become indispensable in her life.

Star was there with Charm and ran up to give her a hug, then placed a wreath of corn on her head, to match her own. In turn, Ailsa presented her friend with a piece of wood. Well, not just any piece of wood. Conall had been teaching her to whittle, and she had fashioned a passable depiction of Charm, fast asleep. It could have been any fat, hairy cat, really, but Star immediately shouted 'Charm!' and gave her another hug, tears threatening to spill from her eyes in typical Star-fashion.

Charm, who had undergone a personality transplant over these last couple of months, now rubbed herself around Ailsa's legs, purring loudly. Was that a smile on her face? It certainly looked better than the snarls she used to get from the previous incarnation of Charm(less).

Conall strolled around the place, playing his beautiful music and drawing admiring glances as he went. She was happy to note that he had eyes for no one but her.

They had settled into a way of life which suited them. They were mostly together here or at Conall's or occasionally apart. It seemed to suit both their individual personalities and their ideas of freedom. She knew he needed communion with nature and the wild and she accepted it completely. All she knew was that they loved each other and to both of them, that was all that mattered.

The proceedings had been started to reinstate Chanter's Hill to Ailsa's land. It was all going well and she had been assured that, because the original 'land-grab' was illegal anyway, full ownership would be regained shortly. For the time being, it had protected status, officially because of owls nesting there. For Sylvia and certain others, though, it was ready for when it might be needed again for 'other' purposes.

She was also advised to seek protected status for it as an ancient tomb, which could not be dug up or changed in any way. She had decided against an archaeological dig to determine the ages of any bones found there. She wanted to let the dead rest in peace.

On the front of Nightowl's Hide was a large blue plaque. It read:

'Nightowl's Hide was where Euphemia Bothwell, known as Effie, hid from the Witch Hunters, along with Lilith, her barn owl and protector. As a direct result of their bigotry, cruelty and persecution, she died. This plaque honours her and her compassion as a Healer. Yet it is also a tribute to all of the so-called witches who were put to death because of the intolerance of their fellow men. We remember them all with the dignity and respect they deserve.'

Acknowledgements

I must mention, above all, the pretty North Yorkshire village of Hutton-le-Hole, on which my village of Hatton-le-Hollow is based.

The 'Hole' in the name is thought to refer to ancient burial 'hollows' on the moors nearby.

The land behind Ailsa's Nightowl's Hide is based on the Ryedale Folk Museum land in the village – a must-see if ever you visit the area. It contains information on the three 'real' witches mentioned in this book – Peggy Devell, Nan Scaife and Emma Todd.

It is only the land area itself that the book is based on, not the many buildings there, but I have retained an important one - the Iron Age Roundhouse.

This reconstructed roundhouse always makes a deep impression on me, so I have made it part of the story.

The Falcon public house is based on The Crown, next to the museum, where my daughter and I have stayed.

Weaver's Green is fictitious but based on Goathland village. It is also the title of one of my earlier books.

Pickering is a real market town in North Yorkshire.

Chanter's Hill itself is fictitious, as is Nightowl's Hide.

The characters in the book are not based on anyone in the village – or indeed anyone that I know or know of.

Farstone is fictitious, with only the location itself based on the village of Levisham, not too far away from Hutton-le-Hole.

I must thank Debbi of the Mystic Spellpot shop once more for the advice she gave me on covens. I have used parts of some real spells here, but they are mostly created by me, including Ailsa's spell, so if they don't work, don't blame me!

I listened to folk music as I wrote Chanter's Hill, notably Steeleye Span, to put me in the 'mood' to write about this music with its historical traditions.

For research, I took a couple of online certificated courses. They were A History of Witches and Magic in England and a Green Witchcraft course. So I am now fully certified (don't you dare…) in these courses. So there…!

Yorkshire escaped most of the Witch hunts, so I have used artistic license occasionally. Although there were a few witch trials around York, there was only one state-sanctioned witch burning there, with one more being hanged.

The persecution of witches remains one of the great injustices of history.

Disclaimer

This is a work of fiction and any resemblance between people, places and events is entirely coincidental unless otherwise stated. Any mistakes with information are mine. Any of the views held by the characters are not necessarily my own.

Printed in Dunstable, United Kingdom